"I want you to come back to me," Leandros said.

Eliana heard his words, but they did not register. It was impossible that they should do so. Her expression, veiled as it was, froze.

"I am quite serious," he said. His eyes were on her, like weights. A weight she could not bear.

"You can't possibly be," she heard herself say, her voice faint, hardly audible.

A new expression crossed his face. Cynical. She could see it in the slight twist to his mouth, the acid look in his eyes. Eyes so dark, so drowning...

"And yet I am," he returned.

He reached for his wineglass, took a hefty slug, then resumed his regard of her.

"Don't get ideas, however," he said. His voice had the same acidity as his eyes. "I want something a lot, lot more limited."

Julia James lives in England and adores the peaceful verdant countryside and the wild shores of Cornwall. She also loves the Mediterranean—so rich in myth and history, with its sunbaked landscapes and olive groves, ancient ruins and azure seas. "The perfect setting for romance!" she says. "Rivaled only by the lush tropical heat of the Caribbean—palms swaying by a silver-sand beach lapped by turquoise waters... What more could lovers want?"

Books by Julia James

Harlequin Presents

Billionaire's Mediterranean Proposal
Irresistible Bargain with the Greek
The Greek's Duty-Bound Royal Bride
The Greek's Penniless Cinderella
Cinderella in the Boss's Palazzo
Cinderella's Baby Confession
Destitute Until the Italian's Diamond
The Cost of Cinderella's Confession
Reclaimed by His Billion-Dollar Ring
Contracted as the Italian's Bride
The Heir She Kept from the Billionaire

Visit the Author Profile page
at Harlequin.com for more titles.

GREEK'S TEMPORARY CINDERELLA

JULIA JAMES

PRESENTS

Harlequin®
PRESENTS™

ISBN-13: 978-1-335-93916-6

Greek's Temporary Cinderella

Copyright © 2024 by Julia James

Harlequin Enterprises ULC
22 Adelaide St. West, 41st Floor
Toronto, Ontario M5H 4E3, Canada
www.Harlequin.com

Printed in Lithuania

MIX
Paper | Supporting responsible forestry
FSC® C021394

GREEK'S TEMPORARY CINDERELLA

For HB

CHAPTER ONE

LEANDROS KASTELLANOS NODDED at familiar faces, exchanging civil pleasantries as he made away across the crowded function room at this top Athens hotel, popular with those wanting to throw a lavish party, as was the case tonight. All around, Athens high society was mingling and enjoying itself, the men all in tuxes, as was he himself, and the women all in evening gowns, glittering with jewels.

He was here only because he'd returned unexpectedly early from a business trip to New York, and out of civility to his hosts, the parents of the newly engaged couple whose betrothal party this was.

His expression tightened. He wished the couple well— but not all engagements led to a happy-ever-after marriage...

He should know...

No! He pulled his thoughts back sharply. No point remembering his own disastrous engagement. It had been six long years ago—in the past. A past he had no interest in revisiting. He was no longer the fool he'd been at twenty-six, swept away on a tide of romance. Blinding himself to the true nature of the woman he had fallen so hard for.

Until he'd seen her true nature for himself—had his face slammed into it.

It wasn't me she loved—it was the Kastellanos money.

And if that wasn't going to be coming her way—well, she was off. Dumping me faster than you could say—as his father had spelt out to her—disinherited.

The realisation had been brutal.

My faithless fiancée.

Bitterness filled him. So much for love.

Hadn't his father warned him? And been proved right?

Now, though, the Kastellanos millions were all his anyway. His father's untimely death three years ago had left him one of the richest men in Greece—and the most eligible. But marriage was not on his agenda; he stuck to the kind of passing liaisons in which he had indulged in his youth—before he had been beguiled by the oh-so-deceptive and deceiving *ingénue* beauty of the woman who had proved so faithless.

The function room opened on to a spacious roof terrace, set up for dancing later on. On impulse, he stepped out, wanting to clear his unwelcome thoughts, his toxic memories. The ever-present illuminated Parthenon was visible atop the distant Acropolis and the festoons of hanging lamps around the dance floor cast a soft glow.

The scent of flowers from all the lavishly filled planters at the perimeter of the terrace caught at him.

And one more thing caught at him.

On the far side of the terrace, half in shadow, against the dark foliage, was the pale, slender outline of a woman.

For a second—an instant—time ceased. Then it crashed and crushed him.

Eliana saw him. Saw him step through onto the deserted terrace.

Cold dismay seared through her.

Oh, dear God in heaven, no, no, *no*!

She'd been deeply reluctant to show up here at all—to show up anywhere in Athens!—but Chloe had been adamant.

'You can't hide for ever, Elli—please, please come!'

With deep misgivings she had agreed only when Chloe had sworn that even though her future in-laws, long-standing friends of the Kastellanos family, had invited him, he would not—could not—be there tonight! He was in New York, safely across an ocean.

That, and only that, had persuaded Eliana to show up, out of loyalty to her old school friend. Not that she'd kept in touch much with Chloe since her own marriage—even less since the shocking ending of that marriage.

Arriving tonight, seeing all those faces—many still familiar—she'd felt her nerves get the better of her, and she'd bolted out to the sanctuary of the deserted terrace.

No sanctuary at all—the very opposite.

She felt her lungs turn to stone. He was here—less than ten metres away from her. Imposing upon her consciousness as if he'd been ringed in fire.

The last man in the entire world she could bear to see.

On whom she had not set eyes for six long years—

Yet his final words to her, his denunciation of her—scathing, bitter, contemptuous and cruel—were as clear as if they'd been spoken yesterday.

For a second her vision blurred, then cleared, bringing him back into focus. He had frozen, just as she had—but now he was walking towards her. Striding. Purposeful. Powerful.

Almost, she flinched away. But then, with a strength she had not had to summon for so, so long she steeled herself.

Inwardly, she gave a kind of silent, manic laugh—after what life had done to her, why should she flinch from this blow now?

He came right up to her and she could see the lamplight slant across his features. Features once so familiar. Features now etched like acid on stone. Light glinted in his eyes, but it was a light that was darkness—darkness visible.

He stopped a mere metre from her. Eyes holding hers. Dark and condemning.

His expression changed minutely, and it was taking all her strength just to stand there, immobile, her shoulders steeled, her whole body steeled.

'Well, well—Eliana.'

His voice was like a knife…a blade drawn down her cheek.

'After so long. And as beautiful as ever.'

That dark, killing glint came again into his eyes.

'Tell me, are you here to catch another husband? Another *rich* husband—the only kind you go for…?'

From somewhere—she didn't know where—she found the willpower to hold her ground, outface the contempt unhidden in his taunt.

'No,' she answered. Her voice was cool…as cool as a mountain lake.

'No?' The taunt was still in his voice. 'I'm sure there might be rich pickings to be had here tonight.'

She did not flush. She would not. 'You must excuse me,' she made herself say, her voice still cool. 'I have yet to offer my congratulations to Andreas for being so fortunate as to gain Chloe as his bride-to-be.'

She made to move past him, but he was staying at her side as she headed across the terrace. He was speaking again.

'And likewise I shall congratulate the happy bride-to-be on catching Andreas Manolis, with all his millions.'

Eliana threw a glance up at him. 'Chloe has her own millions,' she said.

'Then it should prove a happy marriage indeed—with no impediment on either side.'

The cynicism—the unspoken accusation over their own thwarted marriage—was open in his voice, but she would not flinch. She simply headed inside. She would find Chloe, then escape.

Escape, escape, escape—dear God, just get out of here!

Her friend saw her, gave a cry of pleasure.

'Elli, you came! I'm so, so pleased. Andreas—here is Eliana, one of my dearest friends for ever! And with her is—'

She stopped short. Suddenly silenced.

Leandros wanted to laugh, but if he did, he knew it would be a savage sound. A snarl. As it was, he leashed his response into a terse, tight-lipped throwaway.

'Don't read anything into it. It's chance, that's all.'

Malign chance—mocking him.

Had he known—had he had the slightest idea that Eliana would be here—he'd never have shown his face. But it was too late now.

He let Andreas's parents introduce him to their son's fiancée, and said whatever it was that the occasion required. As he uttered his pro forma good wishes, Eliana stepped a little aside, as if to increase the distance between them.

As if it were not infinite already.

She was talking to someone else—an older couple, whom he took to be the bride-to-be's parents. He turned away, letting more guests approach the engaged couple, heading for the bar. He needed a drink—a stiff one. Then he'd get out of here.

As for Eliana—

He blanked his mind—blanked her name. Blanked her very existence. Just as he had for six long years. As he would go on doing. Because anything else was unthinkable.

She's out of my life—and she's staying out.

But as he knocked back his shot of whisky at the bar he could still see her, imprinted on his retinas.

As beautiful as ever…hauntingly beautiful…

He slammed the empty glass down on the bar. He needed another shot.

Eliana stepped inside her room at the small two-star hotel which was all she could afford with a sense of shudder-ing relief. She stripped off her evening gown—a leftover from the days before her marriage. Her hands were shak-ing, heart hammering painfully. Weak suddenly, she sank down on the bed.

Oh, dear God, she had seen him again! Seen Leandros!

She had not set eyes on him since that hideous day when she'd slid his ring from her finger, told him she was not going to marry him, and walked away from him.

Gone to the man she was going to marry instead.

Shock broke over her at what had happened this eve-ning, delayed and all the more devastating for it. She felt her tremors increase, the hammering of her heart become more painful yet.

To see Leandros again and to know…to know…

That he hates me with as much hatred as he ever did! That I am as loathsome to him now as then!

He held her in contempt, and she deserved it—that was

the hardest thing to bear. To bear as she had had to bear it for six long years. Since she had walked out on him, rejecting him for another man. A man she hadn't loved—a man she had married only for his money.

Guilt bit at her for what she had done to Leandros—the man she had once loved, whose love for her she had destroyed with her faithlessness.

And she felt guilt of another kind too—survivor guilt. For the man she had married instead of Leandros was now dead—smashed to pieces in a fatal car crash eighteen months ago.

Well, she was getting her just deserts now. She'd married for money, but widowhood had taken that away from her, reduced her to the poverty she had married to avoid. A poverty she deserved, and to which she was now condemned, eking out what little she had. And even that small portion came with a claim on it she could not refuse…

As her thoughts went in that direction they gave her a crumb of comfort. If there was anything to salvage from the wreck she had made of her life, it was that.

As for seeing Leandros again, feeling his scorn, his contempt for her as stinging as it had been six years ago, she must just put it behind her. She did not live in Athens. She would not see him again. Tomorrow she would be heading back to Thessaloniki, the city she'd lived in since her marriage. Back to the life she now led—had to lead—leaving Athens far behind as she had done before, when she had ruined her own life.

And broken her own heart.

Leandros stood out on the terrace of his house in the wealthy Athens suburb of Psychiko, a whisky in his hand, his mood as dark as the night around him. He had left that benighted party as soon as he decently could, wanting only to put it behind him—to wipe the image of the one woman he wished to perdition from his mind.

But she would not go. She was still there, imprinted balefully on his retinas in all the beauty that had once so captivated him. And he saw her here, too—as if she were with him out on the terrace, gazing up at him with those wide-set eyes. And in them was all that he poured down into hers.

He'd kissed her here, on this very terrace, her lips like velvet beneath his, her heart beating like a wild bird as he held her in his arms.

She'd been like no other woman he'd ever found. Till then he'd enjoyed all the privileges of his family wealth and his own good looks, knowing that any female he smiled on would be only too keen to get his interest.

But Eliana was shy—hesitant. Even though her beauty was a loveliness that stopped me in my tracks.

For the first time in his life he'd fallen in love. Determined to win her—overcoming her shyness, the hesitancy born of the sheltered upbringing she'd had—he'd wanted to see in her beautiful blue-grey eyes fringed with smoky lashes all that he himself felt for her. And when he'd asked her to marry him he had seen just that. She had given a little cry and come into his arms, as if she had belonged there all her life—as if she would never leave him.

But leave me she did.

She had walked out on him—gone to another man. Married him instead.

And it was his father who had told him why—who had warned him from the start.

'Her father's financial affairs are seriously shaky. Ru-

mours are flying all over town that he has debts he cannot pay. If he goes under, she'll want a rich husband instead.'

The words stabbed at his head now—and yet he had disbelieved them, right up until the moment when Eliana had slid his ring from his finger. Then, with a bitterness that had been like a knife in his throat, he'd realised his father's warning had been right.

Just as he was right to tell me he was going to test her, by telling her that if I married her he would disinherit me— that our marriage would come without the contents of the Kastellanos coffers for her to enjoy.

He'd told his father to go right ahead—knowing that Eliana would not care, that her love for him was all that mattered to her, not his wealth.

How wrong I was.

Bitterness seared through him again, as strong now as it had been that fateful evening when he'd watched her walk away from him…walk away for ever. Eviscerating him.

He wrenched himself away, heading back indoors. He wanted another whisky. And another one after that, if need be. Anything to block memories.

But they came all the same And just as toxic.

Eliana and me, on that sofa there. She curled up beside me like a kitten, her head on my shoulder and my arm around her. And I was kissing her, and her mouth was sweet like wine, and her body was soft against mine, and all I wanted in the world was to lift her up, carry her upstairs to my bed…

But that had been impossible.

Impossible not just because this had been his father's house then, but also because he'd known Eliana would not have yielded to his mounting desires. She'd wanted to wait till their wedding night.

That ugly twist to his mouth came again. Had that been part of her machinations as well? Withholding her body from him to make him all the more eager to marry her?

He set the empty whisky glass aside. What the hell was the point of standing here, remembering what had happened and what had never happened? Remembering a woman who had never been the woman he'd thought her. Who had made a fool of him…

And then walked away from him.

He had never set eyes on her again—until tonight.

He strode from the room, wrenching his black tie undone as he did so, making for the staircase. He would put tonight out of his head. Tomorrow he was flying to Frankfurt on business, and he was glad of it. Putting as much distance as possible between Greece and himself was the smart thing to do. The only thing.

CHAPTER TWO

ELIANA STEPPED OFF the train on to the platform. She felt dog-tired. She'd slept almost not at all, and the train from Athens to Thessaloniki seemed to have taken for ever. She'd dozed only fitfully in her seat during the five-hour journey, and she still had a bus ride to her destination.

She hefted her small pull-along suitcase, grateful it was on wheels, heading out of the station. As she passed the waiting taxis, her mouth thinned. A bus ride was all that she could afford. Just as her pokey studio flat in a run-down apartment block was all she could afford.

The meagre widow's allowance made to her by Damian's grudging father, Jonas, was supplemented a little by her work in a local supermarket, stacking shelves and minding the till. She would put in a shift this evening, tired as she was.

A wave of depression sank over her. Was this now all her life was going to be? Because how could it be otherwise?

Would to God I had never seen Leandros again...

Stirring up the past. Six years—six *years*—since she had last seen him. Surely she should have become immune to him in those six endless years? But all it had taken was that one single moment of seeing him again for her to know that Leandros Kastellanos, with every reason in the world to hold her in contempt for what she'd done to him, *still* had exactly the same power over her useless, pointless, pathetic senses as he ever had. As if those six long years had never existed.

It was a galling truth—a hopeless one.

I made my choice—I made my life—now I must live with the consequences.

And it was a life without Leandros—a life that could never have him in it again.

Never.

Leandros was back from Frankfurt. He'd returned via London and Brussels, but as he'd come back to Athens it had been as if the city closed over him again. Restlessness had possessed him, and he'd wanted to be off again on his business travels. But right now that wasn't possible. Since his father's death three years ago he'd taken over the running of the company, and it was more than a full-time job. Working lunches, like today's, were the norm.

Today's was in Piraeus, with a couple of directors of a shipping brokerage who were keen on Kastellanos investment funds. Leandros was in two minds about it, and wanted to discuss it with them in person.

The problem was he was finding it an effort to focus on business—ever since seeing Eliana again he'd been finding it so. Try to block them as he might, his thoughts kept gravitating back to her. They did so again now, as his chauffeured car made its way out of Athens south to Piraeus.

He'd heard about Damian Makris's death in a road accident some eighteen months ago now—the news had been all over the press and had circulated amongst his circle of acquaintances. Though it had been shocking—how could

it not be, for a young man still in his twenties to die?—
Leandros had not wanted to think about it. Not wanted to
think that now Eliana was no longer Damian's wife but
his widow.

Jonas Makris, Damian's father, had made it big in construction, and was based in the north of the country, with
lucrative building projects all over the Balkans. That Eliana
had taken herself off to Thessaloniki with the man she'd
preferred to him had been a sour source of what might
have passed for comfort to Leandros. Their paths had never
crossed.

Till that damn party for Andreas Manolis and his fiancée...

*But at least she hasn't shown up in Athens again—I can
be glad of that.*

The taunt he'd thrown at her—that she was now set on
lining up a new husband, rich, of course, the only kind she
went for—came back now, twisting his mouth. Well, she
was welcome to go husband-hunting in Thessaloniki—or
anywhere else that was not Athens.

Though maybe his taunt had been misplaced. Maybe
she was perfectly happy being a wealthy widow, burning
through whatever her hapless husband had left her.

He gave himself a mental shake. Hell, he was thinking
about her again...

His car was arriving at the entrance to the prestigious
yacht club where he was to meet his hosts for lunch. With
an effort, he switched his mind into business gear, running
through the issues that would need discussion and clarifi-
cation if they were to reach agreement.

An hour later he had made his mind up. Though lunch
had been lavish, and his hosts clearly very keen, he had not

taken to them, and considered the deal they wanted carried too much risk for him. He veiled that decision from them—there was no point being blunt when it was not necessary. For now he let them think he would consider it, and they were happy enough with that as they moved on to coffee and liqueurs.

He was only half listening to what his hosts were saying—they were making general conversation about various aspects of the business and political life in Greece in which they all shared an interest—until one of them mentioned a name that suddenly drew his attention sharply.

'A lucky day, though, for Vassily Makris. He'll scoop the lot when old Jonas calls it quits.'

Leandros paused in the act of lifting his coffee cup.

'Vassily Makris?'

If there was an edge in his voice, he veiled it. His engagement to Eliana had been brief, and unannounced—few had known about it, and few knew of his own connection to the widow of Damian Makris.

Her friend Chloe did, though. At that party her reaction had shown that plain enough.

His host nodded. 'Yes—Jonas's nephew. Damian was Jonas's only son—his only child. There's no grandchild either, apparently. Only a widow—Aristides Georgiades's daughter. Jonas, understandably, was never happy that the marriage was childless. And the widow is the loser for that.'

'Yes,' Leandros's other host corroborated. 'Jonas has all but thrown her out on the street, from what I've heard. Of course if the Georgiades money had lasted she'd have been OK, but we all know what happened to that…'

Leandros frowned, before hearing himself ask a question he didn't want to ask, but asked all the same.

'Didn't Aristides Georgiades's property not pass to the daughter when he died? Some historic old place way out in Attica?'

'No,' came the answer. 'Jonas Makris's kept it—it went to him with the marriage. Had his daughter-in-law given him the grandson and heir—any heir at all!—he might have put it in the child's name, but as it is it will all go to the nephew, Vassily.'

Out of nowhere, in his head, Leandros heard Eliana's voice—a voice from long ago—talking affectionately about her childhood home.

'My father loves it—he grew up there, and I did too. It's one of those few remaining neoclassical mansions, built after Greek independence in the nineteenth century by my great-great-grandfather, with beautiful grounds and gardens, and a glorious view!'

Leandros's thoughts came back to the present. So the old Georgiades family mansion was no longer that.

A random thought pricked.

That will have hurt her.

He shook it from him. Why should he care whether Eliana had lost her family mansion? Or that it seemed she hadn't done well financially out of being widowed.

The conversation moved on, and Leandros was relieved.

I don't want to think about her or know anything about her.

He was done with her. Had been done six years ago. And yet…

If she hasn't profited from widowhood, and there's no Georgiades money for her, then she'll definitely be on the lookout for a new meal ticket.

Another thought came.

And with her beauty, it won't take her long to find one…

* * *

Eliana was staring at her bank statement on the screen of her laptop. It made depressing viewing. Her income, such as it was, mostly went out again almost immediately, right at the beginning of the month, leaving her precious little to live on. As for credit cards... She had her own now, with a low limit—all that the bank allowed her in her new penurious circumstances. The credit cards she'd enjoyed as Damian's wife had been stopped the day after his funeral—his father had seen to that. Seen to a lot else, as well.

He hadn't bothered to confront her himself—had communicated only through his lawyer, who'd called at the villa she'd shared with Damian and informed her that she must vacate it, taking only her own personal possessions. And those did not, he'd spelt out, include any of the jewellery she'd worn as Damian's wife.

'They were not gifts to you, merely provided for you to wear,' the lawyer had informed her.

The same had applied to her wardrobe as well, and all she'd been permitted to take had been what she'd brought with her when she'd married Damian. She would be granted a small allowance, and she must make do with that. She knew even that was grudgingly made, and had been done for the sake of appearances only. She had wanted to refuse it, but she was in no position to do so.

She knew well why she was getting such harsh treatment. Jonas Makris had been unforgiving of her for failing to present him with a grandson. He'd been keen on her marriage to his son originally—a trophy wife who was beautiful, well-born, and old money—and the fact that the 'old money' was all but gone had appealed to him, too, for it had meant he could dictate the terms of her marriage to

Damian. Terms she'd agreed to. Just as she had agreed to terms with Damian.

Her face shadowed. Jonas had been a harsh father. She might never have loved Damian, but she had come to pity him.

Their marriage had been useful to both of them, but—

No, don't go there. It's a mess, and that's all there is to it. And now you just have to cope with it.

And that included coping with a financial situation that was precarious in the extreme, and one from which there seemed to be no way out. She'd just have to budget yet more draconianly. Her eyes went to a rare extravagance that she had indulged in that day, reduced for clearance at the supermarket she worked at. She hadn't been able to resist splashing out on it, unwise though it had been to do so. A colourful plastic toy boat—just right for bathtime fun…

She sighed. She'd ask for another shift at the supermarket…get a little more money in, feel a little less precarious. Night shifts paid a fraction better, and as she had no social life whatsoever, what did it matter if she spent her evenings working as well as her days?

But it was wearing—she knew that…felt it. Wearing, tiring and depressing. With no end in sight—none. Just on and on. She was stuck now.

She gave another sigh. There was no point dwelling on it. Her life was what it was. She had made her choice six long years ago, and now she was living with the consequences. Stuck with them.

In her head she could hear again the taunt that Leandros had made, out on the terrace at that hotel where she had so disastrously set eyes on him again, wishing with all her being that she had not.

'*Tell me, are you here to catch another husband? Another rich husband—the only kind you go for...*'

His words mocked her—and condemned her.

She had no defence against them.

None.

Nor against the torment of seeing him again. The man she had once loved, and whose love she had so faithlessly betrayed.

Leandros was at his laptop and he was searching the Internet. He knew he shouldn't, but he couldn't stop himself. A demon was driving him as he typed her name into the search box.

Eliana's name.

Photos leapt on to the screen. Photos from the glossy magazines and tabloids that loved to highlight those living the high life. And Eliana had done just that.

Leandros's gaze bored into the screen. Image after image...

Eliana in a ball gown at some charity gala in Thessaloniki...at a private party on a yacht...at a fancy restaurant...at the opening of one of her father-in-law's prestigious properties... The images went on and on. Eliana with the man she had preferred to himself, Damian Makris. Nothing much to look at—but then his appeal had not been his looks, but his family money.

Leandros frowned involuntarily. He'd barely known the man, but to be dead at twenty-nine was a cruel fate for anyone. His gaze rested now on a sombre image: Eliana without her husband at her side, in a black dress, her father-in-law beside her, leaving her husband's funeral.

Thoughts flickered in his mind as he recalled what those

two brokerage directors had said about how Jonas Makris had all but cast his daughter-in-law out of the family. And again that taunt he himself had thrown at her at that party in Athens. That she must be on the lookout now for a replacement for Damian Makris. A wealthy one, of course.

But not necessarily to marry.

Just someone to provide her with the luxury lifestyle that apparently she was now deprived of.

Someone…anyone…

Anyone who might find her beauty appealing…beguiling… Tempting…

Thoughts were circling now, coming closer like birds of prey—thoughts he must not have, must not allow. To do so would be madness—what else could it be? For six long years he'd blanked Eliana's existence, refused to think about her, relieved that she was away up in Thessaloniki so he wouldn't run into her. Wouldn't see her with the man she had preferred to himself.

But that man was gone now.

So she's available again—and missing her luxury lifestyle…

The birds of prey that were those thoughts he must not have circled closer, talons outstretched, taking hold of him…

His eyes went to her photo on the screen. He was unable to tear his fixed gaze away.

And everything that he had blanked for six long years came rushing back like a tidal wave. Drowning his sanity.

He felt his fingers move again on the keyboard, calling up another tab. Slowly, deliberately, he clicked through the screens, reaching the one he wanted.

Booking his flight to Thessaloniki.

* * *

Eliana had just got off shift and was dog-tired. She'd worked a twelve-hour day—seven in the morning till seven at night—not even stopping for lunch. She gave a sigh as she let herself in to her shabby, depressing studio apartment. Was this really going to be her life from now on? This miserable hand-to-mouth existence?

But what could she do to improve it? She had no marketable skills other than basic ones. She'd skipped on higher education in order to be with her father, and then, for those few, blissful months now lost for ever, tainted by the memory of how they'd ended, she'd thought that her future would be the everlasting bliss of being married to Leandros, making a family with him.

After that she'd been an ornamental, dressed-up doll of a wife for Damien, shown off to his father, to his father's friends and business associates, dressed up to the nines, bejewelled, smiling, making polite small talk as Jonas Makris's docile daughter-in-law. A daughter-in-law who had become an increasing disappointment to him in her failure to present him with the grandson and heir he demanded.

As for Damian...

Her mind slid sideways. Back into the grief she still felt at his death, at the waste of it all. The sheer sadness.

He'd left such a mess behind...

And she was caught up in it.

She gave a tired sigh. Her life now was what it was, and nothing would change it. Nothing *could* change it.

She went into the cramped kitchenette, with its cheap fittings and broken cupboard, stained sink and chipped tiling. She needed coffee—only instant, which was all she could afford these days. She'd brought back a sandwich from the supermarket, marked down at the end of the day, and that would have to do for supper with a tin of soup. Meagre fare, but cheap—and that was all that mattered.

She had just taken a first sip of her weak coffee when something unusual happened. Her doorbell rang. She replaced her mug on the worn laminate work surface, frowning. The rent wasn't due, and no one else ever called except the landlord's agent. The bell rang again—not at the door itself, but at the front door to the apartment block. Still frowning, she crossed to the door to press the buzzer to let it open.

She knew she ought to check who it was first, but the intercom had never worked, and she lacked the energy to trudge down to the main door. It was probably for a different apartment anyway.

She took another mouthful of coffee and then, moments later, there was a knock on her own door. The safety catch was on so, setting down her coffee again, she opened it cautiously—and froze in total shock.

CHAPTER THREE

LEANDROS WAS STILL in shock himself. Eliana lived *here*? In this run-down apartment block in the back end of the city? Had she really been reduced to *this*?

Disbelief had hit him when the airport taxi had dropped him off in this street, and he'd stared around, questioning whether he had possibly got the wrong address. But no, he had not. And that was definitely Eliana standing there, her face ashen, in the narrow gap of the safety chained doorway.

He watched her fumble with the safety chain, as though her hands wouldn't work properly, and as the door opened more widely he stepped forward. She stepped away, as if automatically, and then he was inside, casting a still half-disbelieving look around him at the tiny studio, with its shabby furniture, worn floor, cramped kitchenette and totally depressing air of chronic poverty.

Eliana had not just gone down in the world—she had reached the bottom.

Her face was still ashen, her eyes distended.

'What—? What—? I don't understand… Why—?'

The disconnected words fell from her lips, uncomprehending, as filled with shock as her expression. Leandros's gaze snapped back from surveying her unlovely living quarters to her face. Not just ashen, but with lines of tiredness etched into it. She did not look good…

But that was to his advantage. Just as seeing the daughter of Aristides Georgiades, whose forebears had hobnobbed with the long-gone kings of Greece, now the widow of the son of one of Greece's richest men, reduced to living in a dump like this was to his advantage.

She will do anything to get out of here.

'You really live here?' he heard himself ask.

Something changed in her face. 'As you can see,' she answered tightly.

She crossed her arms across her chest, chin going up. She took a breath, kept talking, her voice less faint now.

'Leandros, what is this? What are you doing here?'

There was blank incomprehension in her tone, but a demand as well.

His own expression altered in response. 'I thought you might like to come out to dinner with me,' he said.

She stared. 'Are you mad?'

He ignored the voice that was telling him that, yes, he was in fact mad to be doing what he was doing. 'I have something I want to speak to you about,' he said instead.

Her face closed. 'So, speak.'

'Not here,' he said dismissively. 'I'll tell you over dinner. It could be…' his voice became silky '…to your advantage.' His gaze flicked around the dump she lived in—had been reduced to living in. 'I could get you out of here,' he said.

Something moved in her eyes—a longing so intense it overrode everything else in her tired face. For a moment he felt pity for her—then he pushed it aside. It wasn't the emotion he intended to feel. As for love—she had killed that six years ago. Now all he wanted from her was something else. Something that had nothing to do with love.

He saw her handbag—a cheap one—on the table, and handed it to her, along with the apartment keys beside it.

'Let's go,' he said.

She seemed totally dazed, and he took advantage of it, guiding her out of the apartment, ushering her downstairs, and into the waiting taxi, which promptly drove off. She sank into her seat, still looking blitzed. But then, he was blitzed too.

All the way up to Thessaloniki a voice inside him had told him that what he was doing was madness. But he was doing it all the same...

He stole a glance at her, sitting silent and immobile, staring ahead blankly. He felt something move within him that was confirming of his mad impulse to come to Thessaloniki like this. For all the tiredness in her eyes, the cheapness of her clothes, her face with not a scrap of make-up, her hair caught back in a straggling knot, her beauty was undimmed.

He let his gaze rest lingeringly on her. She might be beaten down by her new poverty, but she was unbowed.

An air of unreality hit him—was he really sitting here in a taxi with Eliana? Or would he blink and wake up? Find it was only a dream after all?

His expression hardened. He was done with dreams about Eliana. She'd destroyed them six years again—ripped them from him and trampled them into the mire. Now what he wanted from her was a lot more basic.

The taxi made its way out on to the seafront of the city, where there were any number of restaurants—Thessaloniki was the foodie capital of Greece. But tonight was not for gourmet dining—Eliana was hardly dressed for it—and the mid-range fish restaurant the taxi driver had recommended would do fine.

It was quiet at this early hour of the evening, and he chose a table far from the few other diners. Eliana was focussing on her menu, and Leandros knew she was doing so to avoid looking at him.

'Made your decision?' he asked.

She gave a start, naming one of the fish dishes, then looking away again. Leandros beckoned the waiter over, relayed their order, then ordered water, beer for himself, and a carafe of house red. The waiter headed off, returning a few moments later with the drinks order, and a basket of bread with some pats of butter.

Leandros reached for his beer, taking a long draught—he suddenly felt he needed it. Then he poured water and wine for them both.

'Eliana—'

He said her name, and as if on auto-response her eyes went to him. And immediately veiled. Her hand jerked forward to take a piece of bread, which she then crumbled into pieces as if she were doing something to distract herself. She still looked strained…tense as a board. Yet for all that there was a haunting beauty about her. Haunting—and so, so familiar.

Emotions churned in him, but he fought them back. He didn't want those emotions. They were from the past, and he wasn't interested in the past any longer. He was immune to it and inured to it. It was just the present he was interested in—and the immediate future.

'I expect you're wondering why I'm here,' he opened,

helping himself to some bread and buttering it. 'As I said, I have something to put to you.'

He glanced at her semi-covertly. Her expression did not change.

So he spoke again. Not prevaricating, or circling around, or delaying in any way. Cutting right to the chase— to the reason he was here.

'I want you to come back to me,' he said.

Eliana heard his words, but they did not register. It was impossible that they should do so. Her expression, veiled as it already was, froze. So did her fingers, pointlessly crumbling her piece of bread.

'I am quite serious,' he said.

His eyes were on her like weights. A weight she could not bear.

'You can't possibly be,' she heard herself say, her voice faint, hardly audible.

A new expression crossed his face. He was cynical. She could see it in the slight twist to his mouth, the acid look in his eyes. Eyes so dark...so drowning...

'And yet I am,' he returned.

He reached for his wine glass, took a hefty slug, then resumed his regard of her.

'Don't get any ideas, however,' he said. His voice held the same acidity as his eyes. 'I want something a lot more limited this time.' He paused 'You'll do well out of it, all the same.' His eyes narrowed, sweeping over her. 'You really have hit rock bottom, haven't you? I'd heard old man Jonas hadn't gone easy on you—but surely Damian left you something?'

If her face could have gone even more blank, it did.

Then, with a tightness that was in her voice as well as her throat, she spoke.

'Evidently not.'

He frowned. 'Why not? Unless...' That acid look was in his eye again...that cynical twist to his mouth. 'Unless he had reason not to?'

She didn't answer. It was none of his business, her marriage to Damian, and the years she had spent as his wife. Nor was what had happened after his untimely death. Nothing about her was any of his business any more...or his concern. Not that he felt any for her—that was obvious.

But why should he, after what I did to him?

And why, most of all, had he turned up here like this—said to her what he had...?

Waves of unreality were hitting her...slug after slug. How could she be here, sitting opposite Leandros, out of nowhere—absolutely nowhere? For all the desperate blankness in her eyes, they were still fastened on him. Her senses reeling.

Leandros—here—physically so close—

His face...the once so familiar features. His sable hair, his dark and gold-flecked eyes, the line of his jaw, his sculpted mouth, the breadth of his shoulders, the lean strength of his body... All here... All real...

She felt faint with it—with the scent of his aftershave, still the same as she remembered...

Jerkily, she reached for her wine. She needed it.

His face had tightened.

'Looks like you got your just desserts,' he said now, as she stayed silent. 'You married him for money, and now you haven't got it.'

She still said nothing. There was nothing she could or would tell him.

Their food was arriving and she was grateful. Hungrily, she got stuck into her fish, and Leandros did too.

'So, my offer to you...' he opened, as he started eating. 'I want you to come to Paris with me.'

His voice was brisk, without expression. But Eliana stopped eating, eyes fastening on him. Emotion knifed through her before she could stop it.

Paris—the destination that had been going to be their honeymoon...

Leandros was still speaking in that brisk, expressionless tone of voice.

'I have to go there on business next week. I want you to come with me.'

His eyes lifted from his food, looked straight at her. There was a glint in them that was like acid on her skin.

'We'd planned to honeymoon there, remember?'

Her hold on her fork tightened. His eyes were resting on her. Unreadable. But the feel of acid on her skin ate through her.

'We won't be recapturing the past, Eliana,' he went on. 'We'll be...updating it to our current circumstances.'

He ate some more of his fish, washing it down with some wine. He looked across at her again.

'And in these present circumstances I think my offer to you is entirely...appropriate. I am willing to take you on. It will suit us both. I'll provide you with a new wardrobe, and when we part I'll be generous. You will have enough to get you out of the dump you live in, get you back to Athens all fixed up to go husband-hunting again. Just what you want. As for me... Well, I'll get what I want too, Eliana.'

She set down her fork. Looked straight at him.

'Which is what, Leandros?'

Her voice was flat.

A dark, saturnine glint showed in the depths of his night-dark eyes.

'What I was denied, Eliana,' he said softly. 'What you denied me.'

He set his cutlery down too. Reached a hand forward. Folded it over hers still resting over her fork. It felt warm, but like a weight that would crush her to pieces.

Faintness drummed through her.

'You in my bed.'

He had said it. Spelt it out. Laid it out. Bluntly, coarsely, brutally. No hearts and flowers—they had rotted years ago—nothing but the blunt, visceral truth.

He lifted his hand away. The hand that had not touched her for six long years.

'You denied me during our courtship—prating on about wedding nights and so forth. Were you already hedging your bets, even then? Just in case a better offer came along and you wanted to go as a virgin to his bed? I assume you did with Damian? Did he appreciate it, I wonder? Appreciate all your fantastic beauty? Well, whatever... I most definitely *will*. I set no prize on virginity—that would be hypocritical, wouldn't it? Even when I wanted to marry you it was your choice, not mine, to wait until our wedding night—whatever your reason for it. Now, we'll be... let us say "equal" in that respect. Both experienced. We'll make, I am confident, good lovers.'

He went back to eating. The fish was good, tasty and filling. And his mood was improving, his confidence in his own decision increasing. He confirmed it to himself. For six years he'd done his best to ignore the continuing existence of the woman who had once meant all the world to him—now he was going to reverse that policy.

But on his own terms this time. Not hers.

'I'm due in Paris tomorrow. I propose I fly up here again then, and we'll fly to Paris from here. Don't bother packing—we'll hit the fashion houses first thing. Give me your current phone number and I'll text you the time you'll need to be at the airport.'

He was being brisk and businesslike, and he was glad of it. He looked across at her, waiting for her reply. She'd picked up her cutlery again, and was absorbed, it seemed, in eating her own fish.

'Eliana?' he prompted.

She didn't look up, and he waited a moment longer.

'Do you require something on account? Is that it?' he said. 'If so, I expect I can run to that.' He reached into his jacket pocket and took out his wallet. 'If you have expenses here to settle, will this cover it?'

He extracted a few hundred-euro notes and put them by her place.

She stopped eating. Pushed them away from her. Looked across at him.

'Thank you, but no,' she said politely. 'And thank you,' she went on, in the same polite voice, 'but no, in fact, to your kind invitation to go to Paris with you and keep you company in bed.'

He paused again. Then: 'Why not?' He kept his tone casual.

'The past is gone, Leandros. I don't want to try and exhume it. What would be the point?'

'The point, Eliana,' he spelt out deliberately, 'is what I have already said. I will bankroll you, get you back on your feet. You'll be able to start again—look for another rich man to marry you. You can't do that,' he said, and his voice was drier than ever, 'from some dump in a backstreet in Thessaloniki.'

He drained his glass of wine and went on eating, as did she. For all its non-gourmet status, the food was good, and he ate with a will now. He didn't say anything more—he'd let Eliana think over what he'd offered her.

When they'd both finished eating, he settled the bill, then got to his feet.

Leandros was guiding her outside, into the warm air. The seafront stretched along the wide bay. City-dwellers were making their evening *volta*, strolling along—a familiar scene at this hour of the day along every seafront in Greece.

'Let's walk a bit,' he said to her.

Passively, she fell into step beside him. She was still in a daze, unable to believe what was happening. That Leandros had reappeared like this—and what he'd said to her.

Unbelievable.

Unbelievable that he should have said it—or thought she might agree.

Suddenly, he spoke.

'We used to do this every evening—do you remember? In Chania, walking along the curve of the harbour that time when we went to Crete?'

Eliana felt her heart catch. How could she not remember her hand being held fast in his, as if he would never let her go?

But it was me who let him go—went to another man.

Pain—so familiar, so impossible to relinquish—stabbed at her for what she'd done.

'That was a good holiday...'

Leandros was speaking again. There was reminiscence in his voice, but then it changed to hold wry humour.

'You insisted on separate bedrooms.'

Suddenly, he stopped, stepping in front of Eliana. His hands closed over her shoulders. Stilling her. Freezing her. He looked down at her, his face stark in the street light.

'Had...had we not had separate bedrooms all the time back then...'

He drew a breath. She heard it—heard the intensity in his voice when he spoke again.

'You would not would have left me.'

There was something in his voice—something that was like a stab of pain. Then it was gone, replaced by hardness.

He dropped his hands away.

'No—stupid to think that. With or without sex, you'd still have walked out on me, wouldn't you, Eliana? Because I wasn't going to be able to give you what you wanted. Not me...not even sex with me.'

The twist in his voice now was ugly, and she flinched.

'Just money. That was all you wanted from a man. Any man. Did that hapless fool Damian know that? Know that if his father had done what mine did, and threatened to disinherit him, you'd have dumped him as ruthlessly as you dumped me?'

He quickened his pace and she was forced to do likewise. Emotions were smashing around inside her, but there was nothing she could do about it.

Oh, dear God, why had Leandros turned up like this?

Wasn't her life now grim enough as it was, without him twisting the knife that had been in her heart since what she had done to him?

'You don't answer?' Leandros said now, cynicism in his voice. 'Well, what does it matter? Damian knew the risk of marrying a woman who'd just dumped the man she'd been keen to marry until his money vanished.'

And something else entered his voice now—something that made it seem to Eliana that he was trying to convince himself.

'I know the risk I'm taking.' Now his voice had hardened, conviction made. 'Which is why I'm keeping my offer strictly limited. I'll lift you back out of the gutter you've fallen into, but on *my* terms, Eliana—my terms only. Be very clear on that. This is the finish of something old—not the start of something new.'

She didn't answer—there was no point. Instead, she stopped walking.

'I'm tired,' she announced. 'I don't want to walk any further.'

She hadn't wanted to walk at all, but she'd been too dazed, too passive, to do anything else.

'All right. I'll see you back to your apartment.'

He summoned a taxi and she sank into it, closing her eyes. She could not bear to see Leandros. Yet his presence dominated her. She knew he was only a few centimetres away from her…that she would only have to reach out her hand to take his…to feel his fingers mesh with hers as they once had.

Anguish filled her suddenly, flooding her with the sheer misery of it all.

I loved him, and I left him.

And what they'd had so briefly in their lives—what she'd willingly, wantonly destroyed—could never, never come back...

He didn't speak to her again, and she was glad, keeping her eyes shut, terrified that tears might come. Tears he would think deliberate, artificial...manipulative.

At the shabby apartment block the taxi drew up at the kerb, and she stumbled out.

'Eliana—'

Now he spoke. Demanding she halt. She did, unwillingly turning back as he leant towards her from his seat.

'You haven't given me your mobile number.'

She stared at him blankly. Of course she hadn't. A look of irritation flashed across his strong features, and then he was reaching inside his jacket pocket, taking out a card case, removing a card and holding it purposefully out to her.

'Take it,' he said. 'And text me your number. Then I'll give you the flight details.'

He was still holding the business card out to her.

Nervelessly, knowing she shouldn't, but doing it all the same, she took it. Then she turned silently away.

She could barely stay upright. The shock of the whole evening was catching up with her, and she had to get inside—get away, get out of his presence.

She heard him pull the car door closed, speak to the driver, give the name of the city's best hotel. Heard the taxi move off. Then numbly, dumbly, his card burning her fingers as if it were a hot coal, she went inside the apartment block, trudged up the stairs as if a weight were on her back. She was barely able to function.

She got herself inside her studio, collapsed down on the bed.

And just lay there. For a long, long while.

Anguish consuming her.

CHAPTER FOUR

LEANDROS LAY SLEEPLESS on his bed at the hotel. On the other side of the city was Eliana…

He was still shocked by the brutal reality of just how low she had sunk. The cramped, run-down studio flat, the whole shabby apartment block in the back end of town—was that really what she had come down to?

Well, he could get her out of there. Lift her back up to something more like the life she had once lived.

He frowned. Why had she not bitten his hand off when he'd made her his offer? Did she have anything better in mind? His expression hardened. Well, if she did, she wouldn't be getting it from him. He'd been totally upfront with her—she wasn't going to get the chance to have any illusions about what he was offering.

And there was nothing sordid about what he was offering. He wanted an affair with her, a temporary liaison that would give them something each of them wanted. She got a ticket out of that dump of an apartment, and he—well, he got what had been getting under his skin ever since that damn night in Athens all those weeks ago.

He stared, hands behind his head, up at the ceiling of his hotel room, but what he was seeing was not that. It was the image of Eliana, sitting opposite him at the taverna, without a scrap of make-up, in those chain store clothes, her hair pulled starkly off her face—and yet with the same unforgettable beauty that she had always possessed.

His mind slipped further back…back to that holiday he'd reminded her of, their week in Crete. Happiness had consumed him. He'd stepped into another world, with Eliana at his side. The week had been magical—and intensely frustrating too. For her kisses had been an incitement for so much more—and yet she had always drawn back. His only consolation—and it brought a twist to his mouth even now—was the fact that she had found it as hard to draw back from him as he had from her. She'd wanted him—and he'd done his damnedest to show her just how much he wanted her! Done his damnedest to show her just how much she wanted him in return even as, breathless and bemused, she'd pulled away from his embrace in the shadows of that quiet cobbled street in the old part of Chania, where their hotel—a converted merchant's mansion—had lain a few metres beyond.

'Let me come to your room tonight…' His voice had been husky as he'd moved to reach for her again.

She'd held him at bay. 'We agreed. Oh, Leandros, don't make it harder for me than it already is. I want so much to wait for our wedding day…our wedding night…'

There'd been a catch in her voice, her eyes glowing partly with pleading, partly with the desire that he knew had quickened in her as he'd kissed her as seductively as he'd known how.

And he'd honoured her plea—knowing how important it was for her.

His expression changed again, became etched in bitterness. Now, with the acid lens of hindsight, he knew just why it had been so important for her.

So she could go a virgin to Damian's bed.

Had she kept her virginity deliberately from the off? In case something happened to prevent her from marrying him? Would she have given herself only when his ring was on her finger, her access to the Kastellanos wealth secured?

Well, now there would be no ring—and all that she would get from him materially, as he had informed her over dinner, would be the couture wardrobe he would provide, and whatever piece of jewellery he chose to bestow upon her when he had sent her on her way, which she would be able to sell to fund her in Athens.

When I've had enough of her.

And then he could get his life back and be free of her—finally. Finally free.

She will never haunt me again, neither in dreams, nor in waking. I'll be done with her and her power will be gone.

A nerve ticked in his cheek, and he felt his hands clench behind his head as he went on staring sightlessly at the blank and empty ceiling overhead.

'Oh, for heaven's sake, watch where you're going!'

The angry outburst from a shopper was lost on Eliana as she made a muttering apology. Her mind was not on restocking shelves. It was like a tangled skein of wool—knotted and impossible, riven with emotions, a tormented mess. It had been like that all week. Ever since the bombshell Leandros had lobbed at her—as if turning up at her apartment hadn't been bombshell enough.

Through the tangled mess in her head one phrase kept

going round and round and round. She kept hearing his voice saying it.

'I want you to come back to me.'

It was incising itself into her ceaselessly, remorseless, by day and by night. Not letting her go. Tormenting her. She'd tried to overlay it, to smother it, to deafen it with the words she'd said to him, dragged out of her numbly as she'd sat opposite him in the restaurant.

'Thank you, but no.'

She wanted to hang on to them—needed to hang on to them...was desperate to hang on to them. But with each passing day they were getting fainter and fainter.

Oh, dear God, why had Leandros come back into her life? Why couldn't he have stayed out of it? Just gone on ignoring her existence as he had for six long, bleak years.

I don't need this, and I don't want it—I don't, I don't, I don't!

She had enough to cope with—oh, so much more than enough.

She stretched up, replenishing the packets of pasta and rice. The tangled mess of her thoughts and emotions was writhing now, like a nest of snakes, and Leandros's voice was in her head, over and over and over again.

'I want you to come back to me.'

She closed her eyes in anguish. She must not listen to those words—must not heed their power...their tainted temptation to claim again in any way, on any terms, what she once had had.

Leandros desiring her...

As she still desired him...had always done...would always do...

The knowledge was impossible to deny.

In her mind's vivid eye she saw him again as he had been at that fateful party to celebrate Chloe's engagement—and then as he had been only a handful of days ago, striding back into her life. Saw that he still possessed exactly what he had always possessed—the ability to kindle in her that flame of desire.

But I forfeited my right to desire him.

Her eyes shadowed. She had no right to him...to anything of him. Not any more...

Yet memory played again in her head of how they'd walked along the seafront, how she had denied him, all the while trembling in his arms at his kisses.

Guilt smote her again—always, always guilt. Guilt at having betrayed his love for her and denied him his desire for her. The desire he had told her he now wanted to slake...

The tangled, tormenting knot of thoughts and feelings in her head writhed again. How could she be free of her endless guilt? Free of Leandros—finally free? Free of what she had once felt for him? Free of the desire that now could only be tainted by what she'd done to him?

Slowly, fatefully, the words shaped themselves in her head.

If I went to him now, as he asks of me—if I did I could finally move on...put behind me what I did, what I destroyed.

Her guilt would go—the guilt she had felt ever since she had returned his ring, accepted Damian's in its place.

I could be free of it—free of that guilt. Because I would be offering him now what I never offered him then, what is all that he wants of me. And that would free him, too, wouldn't it? He can be purged of me. He can hate me still, but I can make amends—and in doing so free myself.

If she simply went to Paris with Leandros...

All through her shift the thought stayed with her.

All the while she walked back to her studio that evening.

Stayed with her as she sat down on her narrow bed with its lumpy mattress, reached inside her handbag. Took out the business card in the zip pocket. Stared down at it.

She got out her cheap phone and numbly, without thinking about it, without letting herself think about it, she started to tap in the number from the stiff white card.

Sent a text to Leandros.

Scarcely believing that she was doing so.

And yet she was.

Leandros sat in one of the several business lounges at Thessaloniki airport, where he'd just arrived off the shuttle from Athens, drumming his fingers on his briefcase. His flight to Paris was about to be called—and there was no sign of Eliana.

Yet she had agreed to be here. He hadn't spoken to her—she wouldn't take his calls—but she had texted, and it had been by text that he'd told her when to arrive.

So, where was she?

Was she going to show up or not?

He could feel tension whipping across his shoulders. His expression was set, his gaze fixed on the entrance to the lounge. He was oblivious to the fact that he was being eyed up both by the hostess in charge of refreshments and by a female passenger across the lounge, trying to catch his eye. Oblivious to everything except his impatience to see Eliana walk through that damn door...

The flight announcement started, and his tension cranked up even more. OK, so they would want to board the business class passengers first, but there was no immediate urgency. All the same...

She was burning in his head.

And there was only one way to extinguish that flame, that fire.

His gaze darkened. He hated it that it should be so... Despising himself for his weakness... Resenting her for her power to make him so weak.

I should not want her. I should not want to have her with me, to take her to Paris, to claim what she denied me—denied me before she betrayed me, my faithless fiancée...

But it did not matter that he could hear his own thoughts jeering at him—it made no difference. Nothing had made any difference—not since seeing her again in Athens, and then, last week, succumbing to the temptation, to the fire in his head that she had kindled, to confront her here in Thessaloniki. To put to her his contemptuous offer, knowing she would accept it—because how else was she going to get herself out of the gutter she'd fallen into by failing to give Jonas Makris the grandson he'd craved?

So... His darkening thoughts circled back to the present. Where the hell was she?

One of the airline staff was approaching him, a smile on her face and a clipboard in her hand, inviting him to board. 'I'm waiting for someone,' he said curtly, and she nodded smilingly and moved on to another passenger—but not without a lingering glance back at him, to which he was as oblivious as he was any other female's attention.

There was only one female he wanted to pay him attention—to turn up.

And she was there—there in the entrance to the lounge. He felt emotions stab through him—a mix of them.

Anger that she'd run so late, relief that she'd arrived at all, and something even more potent...more stabbing. Something that made his gaze focus on her like a laser beam, taking in the entirety of her in an instant, imprinting it on his retinas.

She was looking fraught—that was the only word for it. Strain in her face, in her eyes, as she hesitantly showed her boarding pass to the attendant at the door, gripping her bag—a shoulder bag that seemed, he thought, to be doubling as a carry-on, bulky and bulging.

He'd told her not to pack, that he'd be supplying her wardrobe, but presumably there were first-night necessities she would need before he took her shopping in the Faubourg Saint-Honoré tomorrow.

He pushed the thought of 'first-night' from him...got to his feet, strode across to her.

'You've cut it fine,' he said. His voice was still curt, and it came out like an admonishment.

She flushed. 'The bus took longer than I thought it would,' she said.

He frowned. 'I told you to take a taxi—that I'd reimburse you the fare.'

She didn't answer, only paid attention to the airline staffer who was hovering, keen for them to board.

Leandros nodded, taking Eliana's elbow. He felt her freeze, and for some reason it annoyed him. But she went with him all the same, disengaging as they left the lounge to make their way towards their gate.

Leandros glanced at her as they walked. She was looking neat, but that was about the only compliment he could pay her. He frowned inwardly. It was...strange... That was the only word he could come up with. To see her dressed so cheaply. Almost as strange—and that was definitely not the only word—as seeing her reduced to living in that squalid rental apartment.

He quickened his pace slightly, unconsciously. Well, that poverty-stricken, squalid existence she'd been forced into was about to change. From now on her luck was looking up—courtesy of himself. Courtesy of the fire burning in his head that only she could extinguish.

When he had got what he wanted from her—then, and only then—he could be free of that burning fire, so disastrously rekindled. He wished to God it wasn't so—wished to God he'd never set eyes on her again. Wished to God that she'd never been widowed, simply so that their paths would never have crossed again and she would have remained out of his reach for ever by her marriage, instead of only six long years.

But now...

Now she was boarding a plane with him, and they were heading to Paris. To have the 'honeymoon' she had denied him. And after that, and only after that, he would, if there was any justice in this world, finally be free of her.

Finally.

'Champagne, madam?'

The steward was proffering a tray with two glasses of gently foaming flutes on it, together with little bowls of salted almonds.

Eliana shook her head, but Leandros simply reached out and took the two flutes with a swift 'thank you', placing them on the table set between their spacious seats. The steward placed the nuts down as well, and then disappeared.

Leandros picked up a flute and held the other one out

to Eliana. Passively, she took it, trying to calm her jangled nerves. Trying not to be so burningly aware of sitting there beside him in the capacious first-class seat. But he was dominating her senses—as he always had.

He always did—always! From the first moment I saw him there was never another man for me. Never...

Not Damian—poor, hapless Damian. Trying to please his overbearing father with a bride Jonas Makris considered suitable for his son—irrespective of what his son might want...

Poor Damian—and yet we both got what each of us wanted from our marriage.

A marriage that had ended with his car smashed to pieces on that treacherous road a year and a half ago, leaving the consequences that it had...

'To Paris—and to our time together there.'

Leandros's low voice interrupted thoughts she didn't want to have...memories she wanted even less. He clinked his glass against hers, a smile pulling at his sculpted mouth. Yet it was a smile that was disquieting. Like the silky note in his voice.

'To our days,' he said. 'And to our nights...'

For a moment his eyes held hers, and then she broke contact, knowing colour had stained across her cheekbones. Knowing why. Because when he looked at her like that...

More memories she must not have came to her. Of how he had once looked at her like that all the time, making no secret of his desire for her—a desire that she, in those heady, intoxicating days of her love for him, had made no secret of returning.

She took a hasty sip of her champagne, letting the soft

mousse fill her mouth, divert her senses from the burning consciousness of Leandros so close beside her.

His power over her senses was as undeniable as ever—and yet now, in the toxic aftermath of what she had done to him all those years ago, he had never been more distant...

Sadness filled her. Yes, she had decided...chosen...resolved to come to him now, like this, for the reasons she had justified to herself and for the sake of the freedom that they must somehow find from each other. It had been her choice—and yet now the reality of it weighed her down. Mocked her.

Had this been our honeymoon six long years ago...flying to Paris, newly wedded, setting off on our life's adventure together...oh, how blissful it would have been.

Instead...

She suppressed a sigh. There was no point in looking back. She had destroyed a past that never was—now she had to cope with the present.

She took another mouthful of champagne. It would likely make her light-headed, but it would provide an insulating layer over her ragged emotions.

Leandros had got some kind of business journal out of his briefcase and was immersed in it. She was glad of it—it gave her time for her breathing to steady, her colour to subside. She helped herself to the salted almonds, feeling a pang of hunger. She'd been far too stressed to eat today, trying to summon the nerve to actually get to the airport at all. She hoped that some kind of meal would be served on the flight. Presumably there would be dinner that evening. And then afterwards, later on—

Her thoughts cut out—absolutely cut out. She could not think ahead to the coming night—dared not. The resolve she'd felt as she'd sent that fateful text to Leandros last week seemed impossible to believe in now.

She felt the aircraft push back, the engine note change. They were taxiing towards the runway. Airborne, she leant back in her seat, closed her eyes. Perhaps Leandros would think her asleep. It would be easier if he did. Though 'easier' was a relative term...

'Are you all right?'

Leandros's voice made her open her eyes, turn her head towards him. He was frowning.

'Thank you, I'm fine,' she said. Her voice was clipped.

'I've never flown with you before,' he said slowly. 'When we went to Crete we went by sea.'

Memory was instant and painful. Standing on the deck of the ferry, leaning on the rail, the wind in her hair, Leandros's arm around her, her head nestled against his shoulder, not a care in the world. And so incredibly happy.

She dropped her eyes, reached for her champagne again. No point remembering that happiness. It was gone. She had destroyed it and it could never return. *Never.*

'So, are you a nervous flyer?'

She couldn't say there was concern in his voice, but the fact that he was asking at all showed something—though what it was she had no idea.

She shook her head. 'No, though I haven't flown much. When my mother was alive we went to England sometimes, to visit the relatives who hadn't objected to her marrying my father, and for her to catch up with friends from her youth. But after she died that all stopped, really. I just stayed with my father, because—'

She stopped. Her mother's death when she was eighteen had devastated her father, and she had centred her life around him, forgoing college, keeping him company in their beautiful but isolated house out in the countryside. It had been a quiet existence.

And then one of her school friends had invited her to her twenty-first birthday party at her family villa in Glyfada, on the Athens Riviera, and she hadn't been able to resist going, even though her father had fretted. And it had been there, out on the terrace, bathed in lights and music, guests dancing and partying, overlooking the waters of the Saronic Gulf, that she had first seen Leandros.

She had fallen for him on the spot, ineluctably drawn towards the tall, self-assured, oh-so-good-looking man in his mid-twenties, unable to tear her eyes away. He'd been talking—flirting—with a sophisticated female wearing a lot of make-up and a revealing dress, who had clearly been all over him. Then he'd glanced across the crowded terrace—and their eyes had met.

For a timeless moment the world had stopped, the music had been silenced, the noise and chatter too—and then, as if in slow motion, she'd seen him turn back to the other girl, smile pleasantly but dismissively, and make his way across the terrace. Straight to her.

He'd smiled down at her.

And she'd been lost.

That was all it had taken—for both of them.

'Because…?' Leandros's prompt brought her back to the present—the present in which that enchanted past could never exist again.

She gave a tiny shrug, not wanting to think about any aspect of the past.

'It was convenient,' she answered.

She saw the flight attendant moving down the gangway,

proffering more champagne, handing out menu cards, and held her flute out for a top-up. It was probably rash, but she felt she needed it. Then she studied the menu, choosing the chicken option. Leandros glanced briefly at his, selecting beef. Then went back to his business journal and Eliana could relax a fraction—but only a fraction. A fraction of a fraction...

The meal when it came was welcome, and she tucked in. For her, decent food, let alone gourmet food, belonged to a different life. Now Leandros was offering that life back to her—

But only if—

Her thoughts cut out. Impossible to think them.

As he began his own meal, Leandros addressed her again.

'So, tell me—which fashion houses in Paris are your favourites now?'

'I don't have any,' she answered. 'Whatever you want.'

'Eliana, it's what *you* want.'

She looked at him, puzzled. 'This is only for you, Leandros,' she replied. 'I'm here because you want me to be here.'

Even as she spoke, she felt her thoughts betray her. Was she truly here, like this, only for his sake? To make what amends she could to him? To do what was still in her power to do—to give him all that he still wanted from her? But not her love—never that...not any longer.

And I will get closure too, won't I? That is all—there is nothing more than that...

Yet once again her betraying thoughts plucked at her...

To be with Leandros again, so tormentingly conscious

of his physical presence at her side, with all of Paris await-ing them…it was not just closure she was after…

Emotion twisted inside her—knotting and tangling.

But Leandros's next words cut through the tangling. Made things simple again—brutally so. His voice was edged, like a knife, to cut through that tangled knot of im-possible emotions.

'Really?' he said. 'I thought you were here because you wanted to get out of that hellhole you've been reduced to living in. To climb back out of the gutter—get your old life back again.'

Her eyes pulled away. The hardness in his was the same as it had been when he had seen her at Chloe's engagement party, that disastrous encounter in Athens. And the same as she had seen six years ago when she'd walked away from him, his denunciation of her ringing in her ears even as got herself out through the door with the last of her shaken strength, her stomach churning at what she was doing. Handing him back his ring…telling him she was going to marry Damian Makris.

She didn't answer him now. There was no point. Instead, she asked some innocuous question about what time they would arrive in Paris.

He told her, adding, 'I'll be dining out tonight—a business dinner. You can have room service. Tomorrow morning I have an appointment, but then we'll head to the Faubourg Saint-Honoré and get your wardrobe sorted. After that… Well, whatever suits us.' He paused, then con-tinued. 'What might you like to do?'

His tone was courteous enough, and she matched hers to it. It seemed the easiest thing to do. Requiring the least effort, the least involvement.

'Whatever you like,' she said.

He made a noise in his throat. 'Don't go complaisant on me, Eliana. You never used to be—and I always liked you for speaking your mind. Other girlfriends...' there was a cynical twist to his mouth now '...they always agreed with everything I wanted—tediously so. You never did, and that was part of your appeal to me—your honesty. Be honest now. So, do you want to do the cultural stuff, or the historical stuff, or just stick to spending my money?'

Only with that did an edge creep into his voice. She heard it, but did not respond. 'I'd like to see anything of Paris,' she said civilly. 'Even the touristy things. It will all be new to me.'

'We can see beyond Paris too, if you like, and if the weather holds.'

His voice was civil now, too, and she was grateful. Maybe if they could just continue to talk in this way, without him cutting at her all the time—*as though I don't know what I did to him, how badly I treated him!*—being with him would be more bearable. Less unbearable...

'What about Versailles?' he went on. 'We had that high on our list, as I recall—'

He broke off abruptly, reaching for his wine and taking a hefty draught.

Eliana paid attention to her food. Somehow she'd drunk her champagne, and now she was starting to sip her chilled white wine. Another layer of insulation over her nerve-endings.

'Then there's the Trianons, too, near Versailles—we could do them...the Grand and the Petit Trianons,' Leandros was saying, back in the same conversational tone.

'Yes,' said Eliana politely, 'we could do that.'

We could do a lot of things, but all you're really taking me to Paris for is sex.

She felt her throat close, anguish clenching it tight, and felt her eyes blinking suddenly.

This might have been our honeymoon together! Starting our lives together. Living our dream together.

But she had made that dream impossible. All that was left to her—and to Leandros, claiming from her the one thing he still wanted of her—was this poisoned present.

Nothing else.

She reached for her wine again. To conceal the tears that threatened…

CHAPTER FIVE

THE PARIS TRAFFIC was bad as they crawled around the Périphérique to make their slow way into the centre. They were staying, so Leandros had told her, on the Left Bank, near Les Invalides.

'You can add Napoleon's tomb to your sightseeing list,' he remarked. 'Our hotel is one of the former grand residences of the city. Once owned by one of Napoleon's marshals, so I understand.'

He was being civil, making conversation, and though Eliana was glad he was not making any more cutting remarks to her, his politeness was detached, impersonal.

I could be anyone—anyone at all.

But how could it be otherwise? she thought painfully. Since she had tugged his ring from her finger, her voice stilted, telling him of her change of plan, everything they had once had between them had been obliterated, as if an axe had fallen. All intimacy severed for ever.

The car was gaining the centre of Paris, familiar from a hundred films, and she craned her head to catch a glimpse of the sights. Leandros pointed them out to her and she realised he must, of course, be far more familiar with the city than she was. She had not travelled abroad much with

Damian—his father had liked to keep him close by and under his watch.

An unexpected start of excitement pricked at her now as the iconic Eiffel Tower came into view nearby. She was here, in Paris, and however...*difficult*...the reason, it was something to be here—and a change, she had to acknowledge honestly, from the dreary, dismal, endlessly grinding impoverishment to which she had been confined since Damian's death.

A sudden yearning smote her.

If only... If only I were here with Leandros as we should have been!

She crushed it down. There was no 'if only' possible. Face set, she kept on gazing out of the window, not looking at Leandros, the man she had betrayed and abandoned. Who would never, *could* never, forgive her...

The hotel was, as Leandros had said, a former grand townhouse, and as they arrived Eliana looked about her with pleasure at the way past and present were intermingled in the luxurious interior.

'We're in the Résidence,' Leandros said to her as he checked them in. 'The main top floor.'

He guided her into the lift, inset beside a grand staircase sweeping upwards, and Eliana felt her nerves start up. The reality of what she was doing was hitting her...the reason for her presence here. At their floor, they emerged on to a wide landing set with a pair of gilded double doors, which Leandros opened with a flourish.

She stepped inside into a beautiful drawing room—there was no other word for it—eighteenth-century in style, with a carpet in rich hues of blue and gold and furniture which, although modern, looked as elegant as the rest of the room, and was styled for comfort as well as elegance. Paintings adorned the walls—again, a skilful mix of modern and classic—and there was a large mirror above the marble fireplace. Long blue silk curtains graced the French windows which, she realised, led onto a little Juliet balcony, overlooking a narrow formal front garden and the quiet street below.

Several doors opened off the drawing room. Leandros crossed to open one of them.

'Your bedroom,' he said.

Eliana's eyes flickered to him, and then to the doorway, and she walked through into the room beyond. It was a double bedroom, with a silk-covered bed, more silk drapes at the windows, and the glimpse of an en suite bathroom through another door.

'Mine's next door,' Leandros said.

Was his voice dry? She didn't know—knew only that her breathing had quickened, as if in agitation, and that nerves were plucking at her again.

'I'll leave you to freshen up,' he was saying now—and he walked back out, closing the door behind him as he did so. 'I need to change for this evening.'

Slowly, Eliana let her shoulder bag down onto the beautiful counterpane and looked about her, still feeling her heart thumping. Dear God, she was here, in Paris, in a hotel suite, and there was only one purpose for her presence here.

Faintness drummed through her, and emotions she could not name—would not name at all. She took a deep, steadying breath instead. The best way to cope with this—the *only* way—was not to think, not to feel, just to keep going, one moment at a time.

'Freshen up', Leandros had said. So she did just that, repairing to the en suite bathroom.

It was a long time, it seemed, since she'd got up that morning, and as the bathroom facilities in her studio were both primitive and limited, the contrast with the palatial bathroom here was total. Almost without realising it, she felt her spirits lift as she stripped off, turned on the shower, stepped inside. The vanity unit came with an overflowing basket of expensive toiletries, and within minutes she was revelling in the feel of washing her hair under a strong, hot stream of water, lathering her body with richly scented bodywash.

Oh, but it felt *good* to have such a shower again—not since she'd lived with Damian had there been such luxury for her.

Luxury she'd once taken for granted.

Luxury that had come with her marriage.

She felt a kind of sudden hollowing in her stomach. And now it was going to be hers again—courtesy of the man she had rejected marrying.

She cut the shower—cut the thoughts starting to invade her mind. They were too disturbing and for too many reasons. Disturbing reasons. Because they were conflicting reasons...reasons she was fighting against admitting.

Being here like this—in Paris, with Leandros—was not simply for the reasons she had been telling herself. Because she owed it to him...because she wanted final closure, so she could move on with her life, move on without Leandros...

She reached for a towel to wind around her wet hair, another to wrap around her naked body. She was conscious of avoiding looking at her reflection. Yet she saw it all the same. Slender...so slender...her nakedness covered only with a towel, her arms and shoulders bare, her legs bare, her breasts pressing against the confines of the towel. She felt an awareness of her own physical body...felt as burningly conscious of herself as she had been of Leandros on the flight over...of the body that soon Leandros would—

Urgently, she tore her thoughts away again. Too disturbing...too conflicting. Just like her emotions. Ragged and raw. Tangled and tormenting.

Impossible to make sense of.

Leandros stood by the Juliet balcony, hands thrust into the trouser pockets of his tuxedo. His mood was strange, his thoughts disjointed, contradicting each other. Had this been a major mistake, letting Eliana back into his life? An act of insanity he would regret all his life? Was he just raking up dead ashes that should be dug into the earth and never exhumed?

Even as the thought came, its negation came even more swiftly. It was his love for Eliana that was dead and gone—nothing else. Seeing her again had rekindled—instantly, totally—everything else he'd ever felt about her. And it was that 'everything else' that he was reviving now—reclaiming now.

That and nothing else.

He felt his heart harden the way he had taught it to—the way she had caused it to. No, there was nothing left of love between them. His face hardened along with his heart. Not that she had ever felt any love for him. It had been self-interest, that was all. The moment his father had threatened to disinherit him she'd cut and run...

But now he'd brought her back into his life. Deliberately and consciously.

On my terms only. For a limited period—and a limited purpose.

To get her out of his system once and for all. It was all he asked for.

The door from her bedroom opened and she emerged. His eyes went to her immediately. She'd changed, and was now wearing something a little more suitable for her surroundings. A below-the-knee dress with a slight floral print, high-waisted and with a blouson bodice. Her hair—newly washed, he could see—was drawn back into a still-damp ponytail.

'That dress isn't chain store,' he heard himself saying.

She gave a little shake of her head, as if his remark had taken her aback.

'No, it's one my father bought me. Like he bought the gown I wore to Chloe's party. They're old now, but good quality.'

He frowned. 'You must have had a decent wardrobe from Damian?' he said.

'I was not allowed to take it when I had to leave the house we lived in,' she said quietly.

Leandros's mouth twisted. Jonas Makris had certainly done the works on her all right.

But I don't want to see her in clothes she wore for the man she rejected me for.

'Well, you'll leave Paris with a new wardrobe,' he said. He crossed to the drinks cabinet. 'I've some time before I need to leave. Would you like a cocktail?'

Into his head came the answer she would once have

given instantly. A Kir Royale—champagne infused with *cassis*. It had always been her favourite.

'G and T,' she said now.

He glanced at her, reaching for the bottle of gin out of the plentiful array in the cabinet, together with tonic water and ice cubes.

'Very English,' he said dryly. He frowned. 'You used to like sweet cocktails.'

'Well, now I prefer something more astringent.'

There was an edge in her voice, and he could hear it. He mixed her drink, and then a martini for himself, coming across to hand her glass to her where she stood in the middle of the room.

He looked at her a moment. 'You look tired,' he said abruptly. 'Worn down.'

She took the glass, met his eyes. 'I'm a widow, Leandros. And I've no money. I've had to take a job with long hours and little pay. So, yes, I'm tired.'

He frowned. 'I know your father died a while back, but surely he left you something?'

She took a sip of her cocktail. 'He had nothing to leave,' she said. 'When I married Damian, Jonas paid my father's debts, but put a charge on his estate. When my father died the charge was executed. There was no money to repay it, so… Well, Jonas foreclosed.'

Leandros was still frowning. 'What about your mother's family? I know you'd said they weren't keen on her marriage.'

'No—they wanted her to marry the man she'd been expected to marry until she came out to Greece on holiday and met my father.'

There was a sour taste in Leandros's mouth suddenly.

Like mother like daughter...

'So she jilted her English boyfriend to marry your father?'

Eliana did not answer him, only took another mouthful of her drink.

'Have you no English family to turn to?' he pursued.

This time she did answer. 'There are only a couple of cousins now, and an aunt who was always jealous of my mother—she wouldn't help. And anyway—'

She stopped short. He did not press her to continue. His veiled gaze rested on her. Her youthful dress, her tied-back hair and lack of make-up made her look younger than her age. More like the age she'd been when he'd romanced her, entranced by her natural, radiant beauty.

His expression hardened. She might have looked like an ingenue, wide-eyed and innocent, gazing at him so ardently, adoringly, whispering sweet nothings to him, but *nothing* was all that he had ever meant to her. She'd walked away from him without the slightest hesitation once his father had made it clear he'd cut his own son out of his inheritance, cut him off without the proverbial euro if they married.

She is venal, and worldly, and material wealth is all she cares about.

He spelt the words out in his head deliberately, harshly. He must remember them—not forget them.

Or I will never be free of her.

The sound of the house phone was welcome against such dark thoughts. He crossed to the sideboard to pick it up. He listened, hung up, and turned back to Eliana.

'That's my car. I must go.' He paused. 'I have no idea how long this dinner will go on, so don't wait up. As I said, order whatever you want from room service. This suite comes with its own butler, so discuss it with him.'

She simply nodded, saying nothing. His eyes rested on her for one last moment. She looked...frail. That was the word.

He shook it from him. He hadn't brought her here to pity her, but to get closure—finally to achieve that.

He strode towards the door and was gone.

Eliana lay in bed. After Leandros had left for his dinner she'd stood a moment, wondering what she should do, feeling strange. Had she really just had a cocktail with Leandros, all dressed up in his dinner jacket, as effortlessly devastating as he always was in a tuxedo? But then, of course, he was devastating at any time—any time at all...

She felt emotions flicker—conflicting, confusing. But how could they be anything else at seeing Leandros again—having him physically in front of her, with the sheer overwhelming impact on her that he'd always had—but for that to be dominated by all that now separated them.

She went across to the sofa, sat herself down on it, sipping her G and T, wanting the alcohol to numb her nerve-endings.

There was a complicated-looking remote control on the low table in front of her and she picked it up, clicking it. The mirror above the fireplace sprang into life—a wall-hung TV. She channel-surfed idly, not engaging, and then let it settle to an English language news station. Perhaps the miseries of the world would take her mind off the moment. So, too, might ordering dinner for herself—drinking on an empty stomach was not wise.

She picked up another handset, placed on the side table

by the sofa, and got through to Reception, gave an order for dinner. She'd asked for something she could eat while watching TV, and was duly obliged, with the politely attentive butler setting out her repast on the coffee table, then taking his leave.

She ate, then took her empty plates through to the kitchen that came as part of the Résidence, and busied herself washing them up. Then she made herself a herbal tea and went back to the sofa. She found a nature programme, and then a history one—they whiled away the time.

She ought to relax. Here she was in a luxury hotel, with nothing to do but indulge herself. Yet she was strung out like a piece of wire.

After a while she gave up on the TV and retired to her bedroom. There was a well-stocked bookcase in the drawing room, many books in English, and she'd selected an old favourite—*Persuasion*.

But as she sat up in bed, wearing the Victorian-style nightdress that she had worn long ago as a teenager, the soft mattress a world away from the lumpy bed in her studio apartment, propped up on luxuriant pillows, she thought maybe *Persuasion* had not been a good choice. Jane Austen's heroine had ruined her own life over the lack of money. Turning down the man who'd loved her.

She got a second chance, though.

Bleakness sat in her eyes. Second chances did not always come.

They can't for me. Leandros only wants closure—nothing else.

And so did she. Surely that was all she wanted? All that it was sane for her to want?

Wearily, she dropped the book, shut her eyes. She had

committed herself to this—to being here in Paris with Leandros—but the more she faced the actual implications of what was going to happen now that she was here, the more tangled she became, emotions meshing and twisting, troubling and tormenting.

She gave a start—that was the door of the Résidence opening. She heard Leandros moving around…heard, she thought, the clink of a glass, then the sound of his bedroom door opening. Then silence.

For a long, endless moment she just went on lying there. Her heart was beating fast in her chest, she could feel it. Emotions, tangled and tormenting, twisted inside her. Wanting and not wanting. Not wanting and wanting…

Wanting…

Leandros was here—so close, a mere room away. Leandros who, for six long years, had been impossibly out of reach, impossibly distant. Leandros from whom, six years ago, she had walked away. And now… Oh, now he was back in her life—for whatever dark reason, whatever bitter purpose… He was here now, and so was she…

So close—so very, very close…

Leandros.

His name cried out in her head.

Without any consciousness of what she was doing, letting some impulse direct her—some impulse she could not repress, could not deny—and with her heart still beating audibly within her, the breath stopping in her throat, she felt herself slide out of bed. Set her feet on the floor. Cross the room. Open the door…step through it.

On leaden feet, impelled by the guilt that had consumed her for six bitter years, and impelled by so much more…by those tangled, twisting, tormented emotions…she headed towards the door of Leandros's own bedroom.

It opened with a click, and she stepped inside.

Leandros was reading. The bedside lamp was sufficient to illuminate the text of the international business journal he was attempting to look at. *Attempting* was the only word that was appropriate. He couldn't focus on the contents. His thoughts were all over the place.

Correction—they are in one place only…

The bedroom next to his.

She was there. Eliana. Real, live and no fantasy. No dream. No long-lost yearning.

So go to her.

The words were in his head, in his will—but he was resisting them. Yes, he'd brought her here to Paris for precisely the purpose that was now urging him on, but with his head—if not, alas, his body—he knew that now was not the right time. Tonight it had been a formal dinner, tomorrow he had his client appointment—he wanted all business affairs out of the way before he turned his focus on Eliana.

And there was another reason too. He wanted to give her time. Oh, she deserved no consideration, but he would allow it her all the same. He would treat her well—whether she deserved it or not.

He forced his gaze back on to the article he was attempting to read. He wished he felt sleepy, at least, not as if this edgy restlessness was possessing him.

And then, as his eyes glazed over yet again, not seeing the text, he heard his bedroom door open.

Immediately, his gaze flashed upwards, pulse leaping.

It was Eliana. Standing in the doorway.

And Leandros's blood leapt again.

Eliana forced herself forward. Her feet felt like blocks of lead, and her heart was thudding in her chest at the thought of what she was doing. But she made herself pad forward.

Leandros's gaze had lifted from his magazine and gone straight to her—eyes fixed on her like lasers. She felt her cheeks flush, then whiten, as her own gaze took in, instantly, the fact that he was sitting in bed, bedclothes casually drawn over his lower half, his torso bare. Smooth, muscled, lightly tanned, lithe and powerful...

She swallowed.

She had to say something. Of course she did. But her throat was as narrow as a crushed straw.

She swallowed again, halted halfway across the room.

Leandros let his magazine drop, his lasering eyes never leaving her. Saying nothing.

So she spoke instead—she had to. With an effort, she managed to get the words out, past the deafening thudding of her heart, the blood drumming in her ears. She felt hot and cold all at the same time, weak and faint, forcing herself to stay upright.

'Leandros...' She said his name, faint and hesitant. 'I... I...'

It was all she could manage. Something changed in his face. His expression was edged...became guarded and loaded at the same time.

'Yes?' The edge was in his voice too.

She took another halting step forward, half lifted a hand, then let it drop again.

'Leandros.' She got his name out again, less hesitant

now, but with a husk in it that even she could hear. She swallowed once more, took another step forward, lifted her hand again.

Was she imploring him? And if so, for what?

'Eliana.'

He echoed her style of address, his voice flat now. The edge was still in his face, and in his voice.

'What is it that you want?'

It was a polite inquiry—or could have been. But she knew it wasn't. She felt herself flush again and made herself speak. He obviously wasn't going to help her out.

She took a larger breath, lifted her chin—looked straight at him. 'You brought me here to Paris for one reason only, so—' she took yet another breath '—here I am.'

She let her hand drop, knowing she was just standing there, wearing her ankle-length nightgown, a few metres from the end of his bed. And he was sitting there, propped up by his pillows, his bare torso exposed, looking at her.

Like a pasha waiting for his chosen female from the harem to approach him...

Dark stories from the grim centuries of the Ottoman conquest and occupation of Greece were in her head. Was that what she was? One of those hapless females procured to serve...to service...their imperial masters?

Her face tightened. No, she was not.

I'm here by my own choice—because I choose to be here.

And whatever the tangled and tormenting reasons for doing what she had done—coming here to Paris with Leandros, coming into his bedroom now—they were *her* reasons.

She pressed her lips together a moment, then spoke

again. Firmer now, more resolute, though the blood was still thudding in her ears.

'You said you wanted the honeymoon I denied you. So now I...' she took a breath, knowing it was ragged, knowing her heart was still beating audibly in her chest '...I give it to you.'

It was all she could say. She wanted to say so much—but that was impossible. All she could do was take another step forward, and then another, as if drawn towards him. At the foot of the bed she stopped. She was so close... so very close. She felt her heart rate quicken...emotion quicken. But which emotion? She didn't know—there were too many inside her...

Something was wrong. His expression had changed and she could see the planes of his cheekbones, taut beneath the skin. A sudden shaft of dismay struck her.

'Ah, I see—the sacrificial maiden.'

His words dropped into the silence between them, into the yawning gulf between them.

He shifted position suddenly, flexing his sinewed shoulders. The metallic glint in his eye was steel. And there was steel in his voice as he spoke.

'Well, as it happens, Eliana, I don't require a sacrificial maiden—not that you qualify as a maiden any longer. I don't want a sacrifice at all—and least of all...' the steel was a blade now '...do I want one who thinks she can assuage her wrongdoing by making such a virtuous sacrifice...'

She cried out with protest in her voice at what he was saying. 'No! It isn't like that—'

He didn't let her say more. His voice was twisted, sarcasm knifing in it. 'Do not think,' he said, and each word was a twist of his knife, 'that you can make me feel bad about bringing you here—that you can present yourself as some kind of victim, required to lay down her beautiful body for my vengeful lust!'

His words were stripping her, but he was going on, leaning forward suddenly.

'You don't get to play that convenient role. Because, my sweet, faithless Eliana, when you do join me in my bed, believe me—oh, *believe* me!—you will be as eager for me as you so fondly think I am for you. Honeymoons—even mockeries of honeymoons, like this one—are mutual. Don't comfort yourself by thinking otherwise!'

The steel in his eyes glinted in the lamplight as he leant back against his pillows, deliberately picked up his magazine. He cast one more look at her, not steely this time, but scathing.

'Get back to bed—your own bed. We've a full day ahead tomorrow.'

She was dismissed. It was as blunt, as brutal as that. Colour flared in her cheeks. Humiliation and more than that—worse than that.

With what self-control she could summon, she turned, walked back to the door. Blood was surging in her, flaring in her heated cheeks. In her room, she flung herself back into bed, felt emotions surging along with the blood in her distended veins.

Was he right? Was that why she had gone to him as she had? Just to assuage her own guilt at what she had done to him six years ago? Making a sacrifice of herself? Atoning for the wrong she'd done him?

Is that the only reason I went to him? Truly the only reason?

Easier to think so. Or was she deceiving herself? Suppressing a truth she dared not face…emotions she dared not arouse…?

As she huddled into the bedclothes, turned out her bedside light, she could still see in her mind's eye Leandros in his bed, torso bared, looking at her. And she felt her emotions writhe and twist like snakes with poisoned fangs.

CHAPTER SIX

'OK, TAKE YOUR PICK—plenty to choose from.'

Leandros was speaking, sitting next to her, as he had on the drive from the airport yesterday, in the chauffeured car now cruising through the Faubourg Saint-Honoré, with luxury fashion houses all around.

'I… I don't mind,' Eliana answered. She glanced briefly at him. 'You're paying—you choose.'

She was feeling even more awkward in his company this morning after last night. She had slept fitfully, her emotions more tangled than ever, waking only when the house phone by her bed rang and she groggily answered it to hear Leandros's brisk voice telling her he was off to his client appointment, and would be back after lunch to take her shopping. The butler would serve her breakfast whenever she was ready.

She'd been relieved not to see him, and determined, if nothing else, to enjoy the luxury of her surroundings after so many grim months of poverty and deprivation. She'd decided she would deal with being with Leandros again when she had to—and till then she'd make the most of a filling and leisurely breakfast in bed, then a lengthy, pampering bath.

Then, dressed in the same outdated frock she'd worn

the previous evening, since her choice was very limited, she'd gone downstairs to explore the hotel, making her way out into the rear garden. The day was pleasantly warm, sunshine shafting across the small but elegantly laid-out space, and she'd found a quiet bench and read some more of *Persuasion*.

Captain Wentworth was despising Anne Elliot with ill-concealed disdain. Anne was enduring it painfully.

Eliana felt for her.

At least Anne Elliot hadn't had to endure Wentworth's scathing tongue. As Eliana did Leandros's now.

'Eliana.' Leandros's voice was bladed. 'I told you last night—drop the martyr pose. You're here with me of your own choice and now you can choose the clothes you'll be wearing here.'

She named a fashion house—one she could see they were nearing, and which she did personally like—and the car pulled up at it. She was left to make her own choices as the *vendeuses* ushered her to the fitting rooms, to emerge some time later with her choices made.

Leandros was sitting in the plush waiting area, reading a magazine about upmarket cars from a selection thought-fully provided by the fashion house for attendant males.

He looked up as she emerged. Eliana felt his eyes go to her. Rest on her. Saw his expression change.

There was approval in his eyes—and more. A light she had not seen before, yet could remember, oh, so well. She felt colour flare…walked forward hurriedly. To see Lean-dros look at her like that, letting her know, quite openly, that he liked what he was seeing, that she was pleasing to his eyes…

'Finally,' he said, nodding slowly.

He got to his feet, his gaze still taking in the change in her appearance.

She wore a belted two-piece in cinnamon-coloured fine wool jersey, gracefully skimming her slender figure. It was both chic and comfortable to wear. She'd accessorised it with a plain but soft leather handbag, moderately heeled matching shoes, and a printed silk scarf that went with the short, lightweight jacket with bracelet sleeves. She'd added some fashion jewellery—topaz beads and a chunky bracelet.

One of the *vendeuses* had discreetly inquired whether she would like to avail herself of the fashion house's own-brand make-up selection, and she had done so. She hadn't used it lavishly, just applied some tawny eyeshadow and mascara, and a tinted lip gloss to give a soft sheen to her lips, finishing off with a spray of the fashion house's latest perfume. She'd redressed her hair too, changing it from the plain ponytail to a stylish French pleat fastened with *faux* tortoiseshell combs.

As she'd put the final touches to her face and hair, she'd told herself that it was because her outfit deserved it. That it was part of her attempt to make amends to Leandros…

But it was more than that, she knew. Knew it when she saw his eyes resting on her with approval in them—and more than approval.

He used to look at me like that all the time. Is that what I'm yearning for? To recapture that?

She put the thought aside—it was too painful, too difficult.

Too tangled.

Instead, she simply said, 'I've bought quite a lot—you said I should.'

He made no demur, merely settled the hefty bill to cover a good half a dozen carrier bags bearing the fashion house's name with the flick of a platinum credit card.

'Now for evening dresses—but not here,' he said.

They got back into the dutifully waiting car, and the carrier bags were stashed neatly in the capacious boot by the chauffeur. Leandros named a fashion house that Eliana knew made a speciality of ultra-alluring designs. She'd never shopped there. It had been too sophisticated for when she'd been young, and not conservative enough to please her father-in-law. As for Damian—well, he'd just wanted her to wear whatever his father had wanted her to wear. That had been his sole concern—not contesting his father's dictates or defying his will. Except, of course—

She pulled her mind away. Gave herself over to what was happening now. This time it was Leandros making the choices, not her. Well, if that was what he wanted, that was his call. This whole expedition was his call, after all. She would not be keeping any of these clothes when her time with him was over. However venal he thought her, she would not prove it to him in that, at least. Even if she could not defend herself for her past actions and they would stain her for ever...

She was grateful to him for diverting her thoughts, her painful memories, by saying, 'Time for some sightseeing— shall we see what's happening to Notre Dame?'

'Why not?' she said.

She kept her voice studiedly neutral. But it was an effort. Somehow, when she'd just been wearing her poverty-stricken, cheap-of-necessity clothes, making no effort to look good, it had been easier—easier to ignore, or downplay at least, the impact Leandros had on her. But now, chic and elegant, with her flattering hairstyle and a touch of make-up to enhance her appearance, she was more conscious than ever of the man sitting beside her in the confines of the chauffeur-driven car.

More like old times. When I only wanted to look good for him, to revel in his finding me beautiful. I thrilled to see him looking at me...wanting only to gaze at him in return...feeling myself melting inside...

Deliberately, she made herself look out of the window, away from the temptation that was Leandros, and away from the memories she should not allow herself, for those times had gone for ever. Instead, she watched as the car crossed over to the Île de la Cité, closing in on the great cathedral.

'It's still in repair after the catastrophic fire a few years ago,' Leandros was saying. 'But we can look at the outside. Would you care for that?'

'Why not?' said Eliana again.

They got out, walking on to the great concourse by the west front. It was milling with tourists, and there were plenty of noticeboards showing the extent of the original damage and what was being done to restore it. She saw Leandros gazing up at the solid, four-square towers, at the Romanesque arch between them with its ornate carvings.

'I first came here with my father,' he said. 'We went up on to the roof, saw the gargoyles. Great for a twelve-year-old.'

There was a fond, reminiscent note to his voice. He had been close to his father, Eliana knew. Although their fathers had been very different, it was something she and Leandros had had in common, and they'd talked about it sometimes. Unlike her, sadly, Leandros had no memories of his mother—she had died when he was a baby.

He glanced at her now. 'I know your father didn't like travelling, and his health was not great, but why didn't you take off as a teenager, Eliana? Do Europe with your friends?'

She wondered why he was bothering to ask, but she answered all the same.

'My father would have worried about me,' she said. 'And I didn't want to leave him.'

'You were very sheltered,' he said slowly. 'Cossetted.'

His eyes were resting on her, and what she saw in them hurt.

'I didn't think you were spoilt, simply…naive. Entitled, I suppose, but not really realising it. I didn't think it mattered. As my wife, you'd have everything you could want, so what would it matter if you'd grown up taking that for granted, expecting to go on being looked after, cossetted, for the rest of your life?' His voice changed, hardened. 'How wrong I was.'

Eliana was silent. What could she say? Nothing in her defence—nothing at all. Instead, she started to walk away a little, as if studying some other aspect of the cathedral. But she was taking little of it in.

He thought me entitled, but after the desolation of losing my mother, my father feared me leaving home, leaving him. It made him shower me with gifts and protect me, which I let him do because I knew it gave him comfort to do so… made him feel…safe. Just as I knew that he was glad that, since I was so keen on marrying, at least it was to someone who would be based in Athens, not too far away.

It was painful to remember…painful to think that. And

pointless too. Her father was dead, and she had never married Leandros...

Leandros came up to her.

'The crypt is open, if you wanted to visit? Otherwise I was going to suggest Sainte-Chapelle—it's a short walk from here, and we can go inside, unlike here.'

Eliana resisted the impulse to say *Why not?* again, lest it draw an edged comment from Leandros. So instead she said politely, 'That sounds good.'

Did it sound good? Did anything they were doing sound good?

But then, how could it? How could anything about the tangled, knotted, twisted mess of emotions she was caught in, ever be 'good'? It was a tangled mess—and Leandros was at the heart of it. Confusing and conflicting, jostling past and present. How overwhelming it was for her to be with Leandros again, however painful the reasons.

The reasons she was admitting.

The reasons she was not...

Her eyes went to him now, as they started to walk away from Notre Dame. How tall he was...how familiar. Once so dear to her so that her breath would catch with it, at seeing his strong profile. She felt a sudden impulse to reach for his hand, to take it and walk along beside him, hand in hand, as they had once always done...

She felt her hands clench at her sides in painful self-denial.

'Just along here,' Leandros announced, and she looked to where he was indicating, at Sainte-Chapelle, instead of where her eyes wanted to linger—on him at her side.

Leandros got entrance tickets and they went inside. Immediately, Eliana gasped in awe. Sunshine was pouring through the narrow windows that soared the height of the walls, one after another along the length of the nave, leading the eye towards the glory of the vast rose window above the altar. She gazed, amazed at the sheer incredible beauty of it.

'It's like being inside a jewel box!' she exclaimed wonderingly, gazing around her.

'The rose window depicts the Apocalypse,' Leandros was saying. 'The Four Horsemen are there somewhere, and all the other signs of the end of the world.'

She gave a little shudder. 'I won't look too closely,' she said.

She turned her attention to the painted pillars, as brilliantly coloured as the stained glass, and then to the vaulted ceilings running alongside the main aisle, painted in French blue with the French royal fleur de Lys.

'The chapel was commissioned by Louis IX, the saintly King of the early Middle Ages,' Leandros remarked beside her.

'He was the one whose first wife was Eleanor of Aquitaine, wasn't he? Before she went off to marry Henry Plantagenet, King of England.'

'No, she married an earlier Louis, then Henry Plantagenet of England. Two glittering marriages—a queen twice over. Of course, as an heiress in her own right she didn't need to marry to enjoy a lavish lifestyle.'

Eliana made no answer—there was none to make. If it was yet another dig at her, then it was one he was, after all, entitled to make. She wandered away a little, moving to examine one of the many painted statuettes adorning this jewel box of a chapel, knowing that the sting of his words was both hurtful and to be expected. And there was nothing she could do about either. Yet they hung in her head for all that, heavy and hard.

Leandros let her be and she continued her exploration, wanting diversion. As she returned from her circuit he said, pleasantly, 'Seen enough?'

She nodded, and they made their way out again.

He glanced at his watch. 'We should be getting back. You'll need time to get yourself ready—we're going to the opera. Puccini's *Manon Lescaut*. It should suit you.'

That was definitely a dig—it was an opera about a poor girl who rejected her equally poor lover in favour of a wealthy suitor. She wanted to protest, riposte, find some way of answering back. But how could she? Like Manon, she had chosen wealth over love.

Not that that had stopped her first love from wanting her to want him still.

As she got into the car that Leandros had summoned to their side his words from the night before were in her head—how he did not want her to make a sacrifice of herself. Taunting her that she would be eager for him.

He wants me to want him.

Her eyes shadowed as she pulled her seat belt across. The man she wanted was the man she had once known, so long ago. The man she had once loved—and rejected. This man now—this Leandros—was not that man. And she was not the woman he had once loved either.

So what is there left? Nothing that I want.

That was the truth of it, she thought bleakly. Leandros here, now, only wanted a sexual affair with her—she had forfeited anything more. But for herself...?

Her eyes went to him now, in profile, as they crossed

over the river to the Left Bank. Emotions flowed within her as turbid as the waters of the Seine—and as unknowable.

She gave up on her thoughts, which were as hopeless as her emotions to try and untangle, as the car made its way through the Paris traffic. Leandros was studying his phone messages, absorbed and silent.

Back at their hotel, in their suite, he spoke.

'The Paris opera is very grand, so look your best. Wear one of the new evening gowns. I've taken a box—a *loge*—and there will be people there this evening whom I know.'

She nodded acquiescently, before disappearing into the sanctuary of her bedroom. It would take time to get herself ready.

Memory played tormentingly of how once she had rejoiced in making herself as lovely as she could for an evening with Leandros, taking endless trouble with her hair, her make-up, wanting to look wonderful for him, wanting…longing…to see his eyes light up when he saw her. Light up with love.

And now…

Now it will only be with desire.

Pain twisted inside her and, knowing how useless it was, she went to select from the three evening gowns Leandros had bought her. All were fabulous—and revealing. Designed specifically to show off her beauty—and her body.

She picked the pale blue one, because its décolletage, though low cut, was draped, and she could pin it higher than it would otherwise fall. For all that, when she finally slipped it over her head, letting the silk glide down her body, the bias cut clung to her hips, the length of her thighs. Her shoulders were all but completely exposed by the thin straps.

She wished she had a shawl, or a stole of some kind, but there was only a luxuriously soft fake fur evening jacket, which would have to be discarded once they were seated.

She gave herself one last look in the floor-length mirror on the wall, her expression troubled. Even after pinning her bodice higher, she still felt it was too low. She also knew that with her ice-blue slinky evening gown, her full *maquillage*, and her hair in a sophisticated upswept style, it was almost as if she were a different person. A new person. Not the drab, work-worn pauper living the poverty-stricken life forced upon her, not the jewel-laden trophy wife of Jonas Makris's son, and nor—she felt a painful pang go through her—the youthful self she had once been, romantically gowned, her hair loose and flowing, wide-eyed and adoring for the man she loved.

Now she was the woman Leandros wanted her to be— alluring, tempting, a *femme fatale*...

The only way he wants me to be now.

Her expression changed.

And what do I want to be now?

The question hung there, unknowable and unanswerable, all part of the tangled mess of her emotions, confusing and conflicting.

A sharp tap on the bedroom door made her turn away from her disturbing reflection, her disturbing thoughts. She slid her bare arms into the short fake fur jacket, picked up the satin evening clutch bag in matching ice-blue, and walked to the door on heels much higher than she was used to. Outside waited the man who had once loved her—then hated her.

Now he only desired her.
A poisonous, toxic mix.
She opened the bedroom door and walked out.

CHAPTER SEVEN

LEANDROS STILLED. SHE'D cut it fine, timewise, but *Thee mou*, it had been worth it! His gaze went to her like a magnet. Six years ago her beauty had been that of a young girl, just on the brink of womanhood. Now…

She has become the woman—no longer the girl.

No longer the sweet, innocent ingenue he had known.

His heart hardened. But she had never been that, had she? Not when she'd been threatened by a reality she did not wish to accept.

She wanted me only when she thought me wealthy.

Well, now his wealth would lift her out of the poverty into which she had sunk at least for the duration of his desire for her. Then she would have to make her own way in the world again. He would be done with her.

'The car is waiting,' he said.

His voice was curt, his thoughts dark. Her beauty, her allure, mocked him.

Mocked him even as his eyes went to her as they took their places in the limo and it set off through the Paris traffic for the opera house on the Right Bank. He made no attempt at conversation—his mood had darkened and he saw no reason to disguise it.

There was something about the way she was just sitting

there, resplendent in the soft white faux fur jacket nestled around her shoulders, the upswept hair exposing the line of her neck, the cut of her cheekbones, her always beautiful eyes deepened and darkened by make-up and thick, blackened lashes. Her face was semi-averted from him and she was looking out of the window, studiedly taking no notice of him. All he could see of her gown was the sweep of silk from waist to ankles, her legs slanting away from him.

She was remote from him, withdrawn from him—as if he did not exist for her.

Something flared in the depths of his eyes and he rested his gaze darkly upon her averted profile. He would *make* himself exist for her—she *would* take notice of him. He would make it impossible for her not to.

I want to be rid of this desire for her—dear God, I just want to be rid of it! I want it not to be able to torment me ever again.

It was his only wish.

The car had pulled up outside the opera house, the Palais Garnier, and the driver was opening her door for her. Eliana stepped out carefully, her gaze going to the grand edifice—a legacy of the opulence of the Second Empire of Napoleon III in the mid-nineteenth century. Then Leandros was beside her, taller than ever, it seemed to her, in his evening dress, guiding her in.

The glories of the interior were breathtaking, and she gazed around the lobby, already crowded with women in evening gowns, men in black tie tuxedos. The sheer opulence was almost beyond belief. Her eyes went to the massively imposing staircase that divided in two to sweep to the upper floor with a flamboyance that only the extravagances of the Second Empire could justify. Everywhere there were columns and carvings and statuary, gilded and glowing in the lamplight. She all but blinked at the dazzle.

She felt a touch at her elbow and started.

'This way,' Leandros said at her side.

And then she was being guided up that magnificent staircase, gazing around her as she went. She gathered the skirt of her evening gown with one hand, her heels ringing on the marble stairs. Others were doing likewise, making the ascent to the next level up. There was a chattering of mostly French but other languages too all around her, and the scent of expensive perfume in the air.

They were shown into their *loge* and she stood gazing out over the auditorium, filling up now, and at the other boxes all around as well. She felt hands on her shoulders, and started again.

'Let me take your jacket,' Leandros said.

She was reluctant to part with it, but he was already sliding it from her shoulders—and besides, she was already too warm. Yet with it gone she felt horribly exposed, knowing just how much of her flesh he was seeing—her shoulders, her arms, and the expanse of her décolletage that she had been unable to cover, even with the aid of the safety pins raising the drape of her bodice.

She sat herself down on one of the gilt and velvet chairs, leaning forward slightly to continue her perusal of the spectacular interior of the opera house—and to avoid having to pay any attention to Leandros. Her nerves were on edge, and she was supremely and uncomfortably conscious of her appearance, and of his presence behind her.

She heard him saying something in French to someone who seemed to have come into the back of the box, and she wondered if they were to share it. But then the exchange ceased, and instead she heard the sound of effervescent liquid being poured. A moment later Leandros was standing beside her, proffering a glass of lightly foaming champagne. She took it without thinking, and he raised his own glass to her. The light from the wall lamp threw his features into chiaroscuro, accentuating the planes of his face—hardening them, it seemed to her—and she felt herself tense.

'To my very own Manon,' he said.

His voice was as edged as a knife-blade inserted between her ribs.

'My faithless fiancée…'

She paled—she could not help it. The blade in her flesh twisted, and she almost cried out in pain. Yet she had no defence against it.

She had only the glass of champagne he had bestowed upon her.

She took a mouthful, ignoring the delicate mousse, simply swallowing it down, needing to feel its impact. Yet for all that she could still feel her eyes sting, and she lowered her gaze, letting her mascara-laden eyelashes veil it from him. What good would it do to let him see her pain at his scathing taunt? He would only think she deserved to feel it.

And I know I have no defence to make.

She took another mouthful, welcoming its effervescence in her mouth, in her suddenly constricted throat, as she swallowed it down. She felt its kick and was glad. Grateful.

Leandros was taking the seat beside her—too close, far too close—angling his long legs away from her, then handing her a programme, which presumably had been delivered along with the bottle of champagne.

She was grateful for the programme, which gave her

something to do other than knock back her champagne. She balanced the glass carefully on the unoccupied chair on her other side and bent her head to peruse the programme. It was in French, and she had to focus on trying to understand its explanation of the contents of each act. But she knew the sorry tale well enough—even though *Manon* had never been a favourite Puccini for her. How could it be with such a heroine?

Though 'heroine' was scarcely the word for her. She was vain and conceited and unrepentant, as well as faithless and venal.

Does Leandros truly think me as despicable as she was?

She reached for her champagne again to block the anguished question. As she did, she realised that the house lights were starting to dim, and the audience had taken their seats. The orchestra was done with tuning up, and a hush was descending over the auditorium. The emergence of the conductor—a famous name, she knew—heralded the start of the performance.

Setting aside her programme, she held the champagne glass instead, finding some comfort in sipping from it as the music sprang into life and the curtain rose on the first act, where the hapless lover, des Grieux, would meet the woman who would destroy his life.

Despite the innocuous opening scene, with its cheerful crowd and carefree students, how could she possibly enjoy so sad and sordid a story? Only when the tenor singing des Grieux—another famous name—launched into the celebrated aria, one of the best known of the opera, did she feel unwilling emotion welling up in her as the familiar cadences caught at her, caught her up in des Grieux's headlong plunge into total, overwhelming love at first sight, swept away by so fatal an indulgence.

Yet it wasn't des Grieux that she was thinking of.

I'm thinking of myself—falling for Leandros the very first time I set eyes on him.

The memory was in her head…instant—indelible.

'Donna non vidi mai…'

Never did I see such a woman… sang the tenor, and the joy and wonder and passionate yearning in his voice soared above the orchestra, out over the audience, reaching up towards her.

Echoing within her.

For, just like des Grieux, never before had she seen someone who made it impossible to turn her head away. At that party in Glyfada, where they'd met, she'd fallen so totally in love in that very moment.

She felt her head turn now, powerless to stop it. Felt her gaze go to Leandros's profile, carved as if from stone. Felt, as Puccini's music soared around her in passionate voice and swelling orchestra, filling her head, her heart, something call from her out of nowhere, it seemed to her. And she was unprepared, unwarned…with emotion rising up in her—an emotion she had thought long extinguished, smothered and lifeless, for six long, bitter, painful, endless years.

But it had not been banished, not extinguished. It was still there, hidden deep inside her—and it was summoned now, against all reason, by the passion of the music. It powered up inside her, all the emotion that had once filled her and which she had thought could be no more, thought impossible. And she could not stop it—could not force it back, force it down, force it back into the oblivion where it needed to be—where it *must* be. For how else could she go on living?

For a moment she was blind as it swept over her, possessing her entirely. Repossessing her.

And then suddenly, unstoppably, it was sweeping from her, sweeping away all the tangled, tormenting, confusing and conflicting emotions that had plagued her since the moment she had set eyes on Leandros again, made the fateful decision to come here to Paris with him. And they had plagued her every hour since. Now they were simply gone—as if they had never been. Swept away to leave uncovered, unhidden, one emotion—only one—that had been there all along. That always would be…

She tore her gaze away, forced it back to the stage below as the aria ended. And yet she was shaken to the core, to the very core of her being, as she realised, saw and knew the truth that had been there all along, concealed in the heart of that tangled confusion of emotions.

Six years might have passed—she might have walked away from Leandros and she might have been wed and widowed since, might have buried the man she had married, with tears for his sad, sad fate—but nothing could now conceal from her what she knew, what blazed within her.

What she still felt—would always feel, could never *not* feel for Leandros, whatever happened, whatever life did to her…

I am here with him now, here with him again after so, so long. And though all he wants of me is what he has declared, that cannot, will not, and does not change what I now know—the truth I now know. About myself.

Unconsciously, she started to sip at her refilled glass again, letting her eyes rest on the stage below, watching the events unfolding that would eventually lead the lovers to their doom. Unconsciously, she let the music take over, flowing over her even as what was happening to her inside was flowing through her.

She knew they were the same—that they shared the same name, the same truth.

That however flawed, however doomed, however one-sided, love always survives somehow—impossible though it must seem.

And now she knew, with a certainty that filled her, that it was still true.

Leandros gave his polite social smile.

'Permit me to introduce Madame Makris. A fellow Hellene, like myself.'

It was the interval, and they were mingling in the spectacular Grand Foyer. Eliana was at his side, drawing admiring glances all around. But how should that not be? Her beauty was radiant—breathtaking. Turning every head. Turning his...

He was glad of the obligation to make small talk with the couple to whom he was now introducing Eliana. The man was a business associate, the woman his wife—ultra-chic as only a Parisienne could be. Did the couple wonder why he was with a woman he had introduced as married? He gave a mental shrug. The French took such things in stride.

The couple smiled at Eliana, and Eliana murmured something in halting French, then stayed silent. Conversation focussed on the performance, and Eliana was asked what she thought of it. She made a polite comment about the soprano and the tenor, and then made an equally polite comment in careful French about the magnificence of their surroundings.

It felt strange to be in company with her. The last time had been six years ago—another lifetime. He pulled his memory away. There was no reason for it…no purpose. The woman at his side now was not the woman he had once thought her.

She never had been.

She had stripped his illusions from him—and the process had been painful. Perhaps it was retaliation, therefore, that made him say to her, as they headed back to their *loge* at the end of the interval, 'The ice-blue of the gown suits you.' His eyes rested on her now, half lidded. He gave a smile. One without humour. 'As icy as your heart?'

She made no answer, but a look passed across her eyes that he did not recognise. Then, with a shock, he did. It was a look he had not expected to see from her.

Sadness.

'You have reason to think so,' she said quietly.

'At least you have the grace to admit that.' His voice was terse.

She looked at him. There was still that same expression in her eyes.

'I admit everything, Leandros,' she said, in that same quiet voice. 'Everything I did to you.'

They reached their *loge* and took their seats again. Her words echoed in his head. And the sadness that had been in her voice. Then his mouth tightened. She might admit what she had done to him—but she had not said she regretted it.

And if she did regret it? Would it make a difference? Would I think less ill of her?

Restlessly, he crossed his legs as the curtain rose. He could catch the faint scent of Eliana's perfume, hear the slight rustle of her gown as she slanted her legs away from his. The sense of her presence at his side in the dim light of the auditorium pressed against him. He focussed, instead, deliberately, on Puccini's passionate music and the events unfolding on the stage, darkening to their desolate conclusion.

The faithless woman was dragging the hapless lover to his death, and hers. He should feel no pity for her—none. And yet as, in the final scene, Manon's besotted lover staggered to seek water in the desert in which they were marooned, and Manon lifted her lovely head to cry out, despairing and agonised, against her fate—*'sola, perduta, abbandonata'*—lost, abandoned, alone—he could not help but feel her anguish.

He felt his eyes go to the woman at his side, sitting as motionless as he.

Abandoned and alone. Her husband dead, cast out by his ruthless father, all but destitute, scraping a living, bereft of all hope of anything better...

He felt emotion stab. It could not be pity. How could it be? She deserved none, had earned none. Not from him.

His expression hardened even as the final anguished notes from the dying lovers on stage brought down the curtain on the final act. There would be no second act for Eliana—not if she had hopes of one from him. He had brought her here only to rid himself of her—to exorcise her former power over him and to free himself.

That, and only that, was his purpose.

A purpose he must abide by. Or risk far too much...

* * *

'What might tempt you?'

Leandros's query made Eliana look up from the menu. After the performance they had removed, as it was popular to do, to the opera's restaurant. Unlike the ornate Second Empire style of the rest of the building, the restaurant had been created as a startling contrast, with modernist style and lines—and a celebrity chef to entice those in the expensive seats to equally expensive post-performance dining.

'I'm not quite sure,' she answered now.

The gourmet menu was full of tempting possibilities, and she would be happy with any of them. Happy just to sit here and have Leandros across the table from her. She seemed, she thought, to be inhabiting a new world—it looked just like the one she had been in before, and yet it had changed. Profoundly, permanently. For there could be no going back now, she knew. She had faced the truth about herself. All that confusion and conflict within herself had gone.

Would it make her happy? No, that was impossible. Leandros's justified bitterness was indelible—she knew that too, accepted it. Just as she accepted the truth of what Puccini's heart-rending music had revealed to her. The truth about herself.

She let her gaze rest on Leandros, feeling again that upwelling of emotion that had come over her, accepting that truth—welcoming it. She was happy just to be here with him, discussing their dining options in the busy restaurant, with chatter and conversation all around them, other diners enjoying the gourmet offerings just as she and Leandros were about to do.

'I'm having the lamb,' Leandros was saying now. 'I recommend it.'

'Then, yes, the lamb,' she agreed, setting aside the menu and agreeing, too, to his recommendation of a salmon and seafood first course.

He was back to being civil to her—no more cutting remarks likening her to Manon. She was glad of it, but she knew now that the pain it caused her did not matter any longer. His bitterness against her was as justified as ever— how could it not be?—but she knew she could not change that. Accepted that she could not. It was only she who had changed, not him, with her new self-knowledge, her new self-awareness. She was no longer confused, or denying, or conflicted. Only clear and certain.

As they dined, they made conversation, as they had that afternoon. Careful, yes, and civil, about neutral matters— the sights of Paris, what was of interest, history and art. Yet all the time she was aware of his eyes lingering on her as he reached for his wine, as he set aside his plate. He did not make it obvious, but it was there all the time.

She welcomed it.

Welcomed, too, her own answering response, knowing how much she wanted to let her gaze rest on him, glory in him…rejoice in what she knew he wanted of her…

Even though it could never match all that she wanted of him…

A sliver of a needle slid under her skin, but she accepted the pain. Leandros would not—could not—think differently about her. He desired her—and despised her. He had brought her here to Paris for the reason he had told her. That would not change. Only she had changed.

I told myself I owed it to him, that I could assuage my guilt at what I did to him by acceding to what he wants of me. That that was all I wanted. But I deceived myself—that was not all.

But now there was no more self-deception, no more denial. Not any more. Now, as his gaze lingered on her, she knew—with every passing moment, with every lingering glance exchanged between them, with her newfound clarity and certainty and acceptance, with all that was flowing within her, lifting her, changing her, quickening her—what tonight would bring.

For Leandros—and herself.

CHAPTER EIGHT

LEANDROS TOOK A slow mouthful of the cognac he'd poured for himself and taken into his bedroom. On their return to their suite, Eliana had made a point of murmuring good-night to him and disappearing into her own room. Leandros had watched her go, wondering whether to stay her. His mood was strange—but then so was hers.

She seemed…different. He wasn't sure how, only that she was. Since the curtain had fallen at the opera she had been different. Over dinner—different. In the car on the way back to the hotel—different. But he didn't know how, or why.

What he did know, as he took another mouthful of the fiery liquid, was that all evening it had become increasingly impossible to take his eyes from her. Even now he could feel heat beating up in his body, filling him with a restlessness that he knew could be assuaged in only one way.

Should he respond to it? Go to her room? Fulfil the reason he had brought her here to Paris with him? Why should he not? She'd agreed to it, gone along with it, so why should he feel this reluctance now?

He swirled the cognac slowly in its glass. His body was telling him—increasingly so—that now was the hour. Her beauty, so breathtakingly displayed in that ice-blue evening gown, had been inflaming him all evening. Yet his own scathing words to her the previous night, spoken right here in this room, saying that he wanted no sacrificial martyr in his bed, that he wanted her as eager for him as he was for her, were sounding in his mind.

But there was no sign of that. Not tonight. His mouth twisted a moment. Maybe he should stop jibing at her, cutting at her to relieve his own bitterness, indulging in his accusations of her. He'd made an effort over dinner, keeping conversation civil, even though sometimes it had been an effort. His mouth twisted again. Not for that reason, but because his eyes had kept going to her, distracting his attention.

He had known his blood was quickening... And it was doing so again now. Tormentingly so.

He knocked back the rest of his cognac, knowing he was doing a disservice to its XXO status.

Maybe he should consider a shower—that might take his mind off where it wanted to go.

He set the empty cognac glass down on the antique mahogany chest of drawers with a click, reaching up to rid himself of his bow tie, loosen his collar.

Restlessness was possessing him again.

And he knew why.

Carefully, Eliana cleansed her face of make-up, taking trouble to do so, making full use of the generously supplied toiletries in her en suite bathroom, then she washed her face with scented soap, patting it dry gently with a soft towel.

She gazed at her reflection, eyes wide and clear.

I told myself I came to Paris because I owed it to

Leandros—because I saw it as a way of finally getting closure for myself.

But she knew that now for the self-deception it had always been. She knew the truth now—had seen it, felt it, faced it as Puccini's heartbreaking music had soared all around her, revealing to her the truth she had been hiding from, denying.

Her hands lifted to her head, removing the pins one by one from her hair, so that it started to fall in luxuriant tresses to her shoulders. She shook it out, cascading down her back in soft, silken folds that framed her face, then reached to the bodice of her gown from which she now removed the two safety pins. Immediately, the drapery dipped across her breasts, exposing her cleavage, the soft swell of her breasts.

She gazed once more at her reflection.

Glorying now in her own beauty.

Beauty that had one purpose only.

She felt a quickening of her pulse, felt a quiver go through her…a shimmering awareness of her own body. With shallow breathing, she turned away, walking out of the en suite bathroom, back into her bedroom. She felt the silken folds of the beautiful gown she was wearing brush her thighs as she crossed to the door, opened it and stepped beyond.

A replay of what she had done last night.

But now, this night…

Oh, it was so different.

As different as dark from light.

As denial from acceptance.

Lie from truth.

Softly, slowly, she opened the door to Leandros's bedroom and stepped inside.

* * *

Leandros turned. He was unknotting his tie, his dinner jacket already discarded, draped around the back of a chair, cuff-links slipped off and placed on the tallboy.

His hands dropped away. He stilled completely.

She was walking towards him. Not as she had before, halting and hesitant. Now she was simply approaching him—in all her breathtaking, matchless beauty. Her gown was slinking around her slender, shapely body, the décolletage low over the sweet swell of her cupped breasts...

He felt something spear within him, and knew it for what it was.

And her hair—

His breath caught. It tumbled in golden glory over her bare shoulders, her bare back, luxuriant and wanton. She had wiped the make-up from her face, but she needed none to enhance her beauty.

His breath caught again, emotions storming within him, unleashed and potent.

She came up to him—unhesitant, unforced, unresistant. She said not a word, and nor did he, as she lifted her hands, wound them around his neck, drew his mouth down to hers...

And he was lost.

His mouth tasted of wine and aromatic coffee, and her fingers at the nape of his neck speared into the sable of his hair. She felt her breasts peak, engorge. Felt desire—oh, sweet, sweet and glorious desire—stream within her. This—*this* was why she was here...why she had come to Paris...why Leandros had had to come to her, ask her to go with him. Six years...six long, anguished years...bereft and punishing... Anguished years she had deserved, yet which now vanished as if they had never been.

His mouth was crushing hers now, and his hands had caught her waist, pulling her against him. Her pliant body yielded to his, hip to hip, thigh to thigh. She felt his body surge, and where once, long ago, in her innocence, it might have shocked her with its sure sign of masculine arousal, now she gloried in it.

He was hers, and she was his. And for this night, this time, this long-deferred union, she would take, and give, and possess and yield what she had never done before.

That all he could feel for her was raw desire she did not care about—could not care about. If that was all she could give him that had any value to him it would be hers to give—and claim. And she would glory and rejoice in the giving and the claiming, now and for ever.

Desire was creaming through her and she gave herself to it, consumingly and passionately, with so much pent-up longing, with so much time to make up for—lost time, damaged time. But she had this time now, and this night. And it was hers to give to him, and to take for herself. Now. Oh, now...

She was pressing her hips against him, feeling his need for her, glorying in it, and in turn pressing her engorged breasts against the hard wall of his chest. The frottage against her cresting nipples was making desire course through her even more powerfully, more urgently.

Without taking his mouth from hers, their tongues still entwining, ravenous for each other, he scooped her up into his arms, swept her across to the waiting bed, coming down with her as he laid her upon it. Then he was shucking off his clothes, ridding himself of them and then setting himself to free her of hers. She lay back, lifting her arms above her head against the pillows, her body displayed for him as he knelt over her, easing the narrow straps from her shoulders, turning her over, sliding down the zip and lifting the pale silk from her body.

She heard, low in his throat, his guttural response to what he had revealed for his own pleasure, his own desire—and she saw it was his desire to have that pleasure. His eyes were dark, glittering with naked desire. His mouth was demanding on hers, his hands shaping her breasts, drawing from her intensities of pleasure she had never known, never dreamt could exist.

Then his mouth descended to the straining peaks, laving and caressing, teasing and delighting with little whorls of pleasure that drew from her throat low, helpless moans of bliss. His hands were moving down her body, smoothing her flanks, slipping beneath her, lifting her hips towards him, his mouth never leaving her silken flesh.

She gave a gasp of wonder, of shock, swiftly followed by intense, unbelievable pleasure. Her hands closed around his shoulders, holding him where he was as his lips glided to where she most exquisitely sensitive. She felt her legs widen, her thighs slacken, as if her body had a will and an appetite of its own. And she could not resist it, must go with it, must give herself to it—could do nothing but be helpless, to crave the pleasure, the exquisite, unbelievable pleasure he was arousing in her.

Desire quickened, became urgent, like a wildfire taking hold of a tinder-dry forest. Her whole body was aflame, her breath shallow, her neck arching, her spine curving, to offer herself...

She felt the pleasure mount, intensify—it was unbearable, it was exquisite, it was all the world, it was her whole being. Little cries broke from her, pleading and imploring. Her fingers indented into his strong, sinewed shoulders and a tide was building in her...a tide she could not stop, would not stop, creaming through her, mounting and mounting, intensifying yet more, until she thought she must surely die of it unless...unless...

And then suddenly, brutally, he was lifting his mouth away from her. She gave a cry of loss, of anguish. But he was moving over her, his powerful thighs parting hers yet more widely, his forearms lifting him now. He was readying himself, poised, and she realised that all that had come before had merely been preparation—to quicken her, arouse her, take her to the point he himself was now at.

She felt his urgency and knew it to be her own as well. His hunger for her was her hunger for him. Wanting...craving...needing more and yet more... And now her hands were fastened around his flexing spine, seeking only to draw him down to her, to let him fill her, make her one with him...

She was blind, lost in a hunger that was a tornado of flame and urgency. Reaching for him, pulling him down to her, she wanted this, only this...his possession...now... Oh, now...now...*now*...

His hands were cupping her flanks, lifting her to him. Her spine was arching like a bow, offering her yearning, pleading body to him, and then he was there, poised at the moment of their ultimate fusion. For one last moment of unbearable hunger he kept her waiting, and as her bliss-blinded gaze clung to his, his eyes burned with a desire that was darkness visible.

She heard him speak—a low, impassioned rasp.

'Now I make you mine...*mine*—'

He drove into her. Full and thrusting and complete.

She screamed. Pain spearing through her like a knife.

Leandros froze. His blurred vision cleared and he was staring down at Eliana's contorted face, realising, dimly, that her hands were pushing desperately against his chest, pushing him away...pushing him out of her.

In some kind of disbelieving slow motion he withdrew from her, knowing his heart was pounding, his breathing was ragged, his consciousness in freefall.

As he came free of her she buckled over, jack-knifing onto her side, curling into a foetal position—protective and rejecting. He put his weight on his knees, staring down at her. In the low light from the bedside lamps he saw her hair was totally swamping her face.

'Eliana—*Christos*!—what is it? What's wrong?'

Consternation was in his voice, bewilderment, incomprehension... The contrast from a moment ago, when he had been blind with desire, craving only one consummation, with what was now pounding through his blood was total.

His answer was only that she hunched her body even more, hugging her drawn-up knees, and from her throat broke a noise that could only be a sob.

With a shaking hand, he smoothed away those tresses from her face. It was still contorted.

He said her name again, his voice shaking now, as did his hand as it lifted away from her. Instinctively, he let his hand close over her shoulder, but she only wrenched herself away the more, and another noise tore from her.

'Dear God—I didn't mean to hurt you!' His own voice was broken, with shock—more than shock—racking through it.

What had happened? What the hell had happened? She had been aflame for him—and he for her.

It had been an instant conflagration as his eyes had gone to her, walking into his room when he had thought her in bed next door. He had felt a shaft of searing gratification at the sight of her, at the clear purpose in her as she came towards him, her body shaped sensuously, gloriously, by her clinging gown, her hips swaying, breasts all but bared by the revealing drape of her low décolletage, and her hair loosened and, oh, so wanton, cascading over her shoulders...

She had come up to him...kissed him. Her lips lush and velvet, claiming his, her hands winding around his neck to draw him to her. And that instant had released from him all that had been waiting for release.

His response had been instant, unstoppable—and all-consuming. Urgent and overpowering—overwhelming. He had been unable to resist—and why should he have? She had not come to him as she had the night before, as some kind of unwilling sacrifice, the difference had been absolute.

Lush and sensuous, desirous and desiring...

It's what I wanted—all that I wanted.

And he had taken what she'd offered, what she had so clearly wanted as well. Every touch, every kiss, every yielding, every low, sensual moan in her throat, every caress and every arching of her body had been an invitation to him to take more, and yet more...

To take all he craved and hungered for.

Until—

His mind reeled, incomprehension possessing it totally. Not knowing what to do, he moved away. He must do something—but what? And how? And then, as he drew away from her, his eyes went to the bedsheet, where they had been lying.

And he froze all over again.

The pain was ebbing, and abject gratitude that it was doing so shuddered through Eliana. Slowly, slowly, she was surfacing from it, and feeling not just the pain, that sudden agony like a knife-thrust, convulsing her, but all the other sensations that had been flooding her overheated, over-stimulated flesh.

Cold was creeping over her now, and she felt her body shiver.

Then the quilt was being drawn over her, and her shoulder was being taken, and slowly, but insistently, Leandros was turning her towards him. Her knees were still drawn up, but she felt them slacken, felt the hectic pounding of her heart rate slow a fraction. Pain—a searing ache—still pierced her.

Leandros was beside her, a sheet pulled half across his waist. He was raised up on one elbow, on his side, and his other hand was carefully, gently, drawing her tumbled hair clear of her face.

He looked down at her.

'I think you need to explain,' he said.

Disbelief was still his dominant consciousness. Yet the evidence was pounding at him. Her scream, her cry of pain when he had entered her—and then… *Thee mou*, that smear of blood…

It isn't possible—it just isn't possible.

She was looking at him. Her features were no longer contorted, yet there was a pallor to her face that told she was still shaken. Her eyes were huge, distended, barely meeting his. But he wanted answers. Needed answers.

'Eliana, you were married for six years—six years! How was I to think—?' He broke off.

Words formed in his head, unspoken but vehement. What the hell kind of marriage had it been for those six long years? Clearly not the kind he had assumed it to be. Had raged that it would be…

And more of his assumptions had self-destructed as well. She'd given Damian no children—no grandson for his father. By choice? To avoid pregnancy? Or had there been chance of pregnancy…? No chance because either she or Damian had been incapable? Or—?

They'd never consummated their marriage.

But *why*?

He looked down at her. And as he did the explanation came to him. The one and only obvious and ineluctable explanation.

'Damian was gay,' he said.

His voice was flat.

But his emotions were not.

Somewhere very deep inside him, emotion was welling—turbid but powerful, seeking entrance to his consciousness, seeking the light. But this was not the time for it.

She hadn't answered him, but her gaze had shifted, and he knew without a doubt that that was the reason for what had happened just now. The reason that, after six years of marriage, she was still a virgin...

Or had been.

Until a few brutal moments ago...

Compunction knifed through him. Had he known—had he had the slightest suspicion—he would never—

'Eliana, I am *sorry*.' His voice was vehement. 'But I never dreamt— How could I? If you had only said... Dear God, I would have been...'

'I didn't know it would hurt,' she said.

Her voice was low and her eyes slipped past his again.

'Not like that.' She swallowed, and now her eyes did meet his. 'And I am sorry too... I... I've shocked you. Shocked myself.'

He saw her start to tremble, saw beneath her lashes tears start to bead. He drew her against him, holding her, as carefully as if she were the rarest porcelain. His breathing was ragged still, but his heart-rate was slowing now, his body subsiding. Passion spent before it even was. But that did not matter...did not exist. All that mattered—all that existed—was his careful holding of her, appalled by his unintentional hurting of her. She was bundled up beneath the protective quilt, his arm around her.

After a while, he spoke. 'Would...would a warm bath help, do you think?' he heard himself ask. 'I can draw it for you. It might be...soothing.'

She swallowed, nodding faintly. 'Thank you,' she said, her voice still low.

He slid from the bed, seizing the bathrobe from the door and wrapping himself in it, heading into the en suite bathroom and turning on the bath taps to full. Not too hot, just warm and…soothing, as he had said. Would bath salts help? Surely they might. And the scent of them, too, would be soothing. What else? What else could he do? Carry her into the bathroom, that was what.

He went back into the bedroom. She was still lying there, bundled up beneath the quilt, still in a foetal position.

'Your bath's all run,' he said.

He didn't ask, only drew back the quilt, scooping her up in one smooth movement. She felt as light as a feather and, naked as she was, he felt her to be terrifyingly vulnerable. He kept his eyes from her, out of consideration, lowering her to her feet beside the fragrantly full bathtub. He turned away, not wanting her to have him seeing her vulnerable nakedness.

'I'll… I'll leave you to it,' he said uncertainly, not knowing what else to do. A thought struck him. 'There's a shower cap, if you don't want your hair to get wet…'

He closed the bathroom door, left her in peace and privacy. His thoughts were still all over the place, his emotions even more so. Disbelief was still uppermost, and things were rearranging themselves inside his head—things he had thought for six long years that now needed to be re-examined. Understood…

What kind of marriage did she have?

Obviously, not the kind that he had thought she had. Not the one that everyone else had thought she had. There had never been a whisper of Damian Makris's sexual orientation that he had known of. But then… His expression darkened. With a domineering father like Damian's, being gay was something no son would freely admit.

Did she know beforehand?

That was the question that burned now. The question he had to know the answer to—*had* to.

Because if she'd known...

Then she didn't leave me for another man—not in that way. Not in the way that lacerated me, carved knives into my flesh...my heart...

His face hardened. The woman he had once loved might have walked into a celibate marriage, but that didn't exonerate her for her decision. She had still married Damian for his money.

Rejecting me because she thought I would be poor and she couldn't face poverty.

It was that that had shown her true nature. Her true character. That was all he must remember about her.

And yet...

Even with the Makris wealth to give her a luxury lifestyle she can hardly have been happy in that marriage. Having a father-in-law holding her at fault for his lack of grandchildren when all along it was his son who had borne the responsibility for it.

Had Damian let her take the blame? Shoulder his father's ire and disappointment?

So that after Damian's death old Jonas had thrown her out of the family, cut her off with nothing?

He frowned again. And if she hadn't been cut off like that...

Would she be here with me now?

The question forced its way into his head—demanding an answer. An answer he did not want to give. To face.

An answer he did not have.

Last night she tried to come to me like some sacrificial

victim, making me feel bad about what I was demanding of her. Yet tonight...

He gazed blindly at the closed door of the en suite bathroom.

Tonight she was a different woman...

He felt emotion buckle through him, confusion and conflict. He turned away, busying himself straightening the bedclothes, tidying the pillows. His eyes went again to the slight telltale stain on the sheet. He should strip the bed.

Instead, he only pulled the quilt over it, smoothing it flat. They would sleep on that. And under the one in her bedroom, which he'd fetch now.

He halted. Would she want to spend the rest of the night with him? His expression changed again with his changing thoughts. He wanted her with him. It was why he had brought her to Paris. Not for her to sleep alone, away from him. Not any longer.

Not now.

He strode out, walked into her bedroom, lifted the quilt up and then, as well, scooping up her nightdress. It was only a cheap garment, with a popular chain store label in it, but if she'd feel more comfortable wearing it tonight— well, that was understandable.

He glanced around. What else might she need?

He saw a tube of face cream on the bedside table, and picked that up too. Plus there was whatever was in the vanity in his own bathroom.

He returned to his own bedroom, laid her quilt over his, draped her nightgown over the pillow on her side, placed the face cream on her bedside table.

Another thought struck him. Hot milk—that might be comforting too, after her bath.

He went out again, heading into the kitchen. He made fresh coffee for himself, heated milk for her, sweetening it with honey, adding some delicate almond biscuits to the tray, carrying it all back with him.

He could hear the bathwater emptying, and he knocked gently on the en suite door, having picked up her nightdress.

'If you open up, I'll pass you your nightgown,' he said.

She did so—just a crack—and he handed it to her, hearing her thank him in a low voice. When she emerged, his eyes went to her. She looked pale still, but better somehow. Her hair hung down her back, a little damp from the bath, curling around her face. She looked younger.

Like I remember her.

'How are you feeling?' he asked.

'Better—thank you. The bath was a good idea.'

She looked around, clearly uncertain what to do.

'I thought you might like some hot milk and honey,' he said. He made his voice encouraging.

'That was kind—thank you.'

He folded back the quilt on her side, gesturing that she should get in. She did, and he propped up the pillows for her, before stepping away again. Then he went round to his side of the bed. He realised, with a start, that he was still naked beneath his bathrobe. He snatched his sleep shorts from underneath the pillow, swiftly pulled them on, adding a tee as well, out of the chest of drawers. Sufficiently decent, he discarded the bathrobe, climbed into bed beside her.

'One hot milk coming up,' he said, and reached for the mug from the tray on the bedside table. 'And almond biscuits.'

'Thank you,' she said, and took the mug and a biscuit. She cupped the former and nibbled the latter.

Leandros reached for his coffee. He'd made it milky, with some of the hot milk he'd heated for her. He helped himself to a couple of the biscuits.

'Be careful of crumbs,' he warned her. 'They're hell to sleep on.' He kept his voice light.

She gave a slight smile, sipping at her milk, easing her shoulders back into the pillows. She turned to him.

'Thank you,' she said. Her voice was still low. 'For the milk, the bath—and for…being understanding about…'

He felt his hand reach out, touch hers. Lightly. Gently. Saying nothing. Simply wanting…

But he didn't know what he wanted. Things had changed. But how, and to what extent, he still didn't know.

One thing he did know.

That to sit here quietly, side by side with her like this, in the midnight hours, in the soft light around them, not speaking but sharing this moment, companionably finishing their warming drinks, sharing the almond biscuits, was good.

And for now, that was enough.

CHAPTER NINE

ELIANA WAS DREAMING. It was the sweetest dream she had ever had. She was warm and safe and tucked under a strong, protective arm, her body nestled back against another body, fitting into the curve of it as if it were the only place in all the world for her to be. She felt herself smile in her dream… a contented, happy smile…knowing with a certainty that was permeating through her, sure and blessed, that this was the only place she ever wanted to be.

Had ever wanted to be…

A happy, contented sigh breathed from her and she snuggled back more still against the warm, protective body cradling her, the strong arm holding her close, holding her safe…

Safe from all the sorrows and difficulties of her life… from all the grief and the sacrifice, all the loss and heartache.

From all the guilt.

She went on dreaming. This was the sweetest dream she had ever had…

Light was filtering through the heavy drapes across the windows, slowly rousing Leandros to consciousness. But he did not want to wake. He was fine as he was…where he was.

Just fine. His arm was over Eliana, and somehow his own body was cradling hers, separated from him only by the cotton of her nightgown. It felt good. So very, very good.

He hovered a while between sleeping and waking, but slowly the latter gained ground, as daylight played on his closed eyelids. He opened them, seeing first the glorious swathe of pale golden hair across the pillow, exposing the tender curve of Eliana's neck. He could not resist it. He moved slightly to drop a kiss on her nape, as lightly as a feather.

Would it rouse her? He didn't know—knew only that her limbs were starting to stretch languorously, her low breathing changing subtly. He stilled. Full consciousness came to him, and the memory of all that the night had brought.

He eased away from her, sliding out of his side of the bed, sitting for a moment, taking in all that had happened. His mind was unsure, uncertain.

He twisted his head, looked back at where Eliana had slipped back into sleep again, lying still. He could not see her face—he had been holding her from behind—only that glorious swathe of hair across the pillow and the tender nape he had just kissed.

For one moment longer he felt that uncertainty, confusion, hold on to his head. Then, with a decision he had not known he had already made, he let it fall away. Oh, it might still be there somewhere, ready to rise again, to pluck at him, disquiet him, but right now...

He got to his feet, walked across to the windows, drew back the drapes. Sunshine flooded in, mild and autumnal, filling the room. He glanced out of the window. The roofs of Paris stretched beyond...the whole city stretched beyond. Inviting and entrancing. He gave a smile. The day looked good.

He padded quietly from the room. Out in the drawing room he phoned through to the butler, ordering breakfast to be served. While he waited he went back into his bedroom, not disturbing Eliana, but whisking away the remains of their midnight milk and coffee, busying himself with the washing up, finishing just as breakfast arrived.

The aroma of fresh coffee filled the air, and of freshly baked croissants, rolls and pastries, along with the crisp tang of freshly squeezed orange juice. He thanked the butler, then dismissed him, wheeling the trolley carefully into his bedroom.

He paused by the bed. 'Breakfast, *madame*, is served,' he announced.

His voice was warm, and his mood, he knew, with a sudden lightening that came as a gift of the morning, of the day ahead, was the best he had known for a long time.

And it stayed good.

And he knew it would stay good all through the leisurely breakfast in bed he would have with Eliana beside him.

She stirred as he made his announcement, and groped herself up into a sitting position, pushing back her long, tangled hair and looking at him. Her expression was uncertain, and he knew that memory was piercing her too, that she didn't know how she should be now, this morning after the night before.

He made it easy for her. Smiled down at her.

'Let's just have breakfast, shall we?' he said.

And in those words were words unspoken—words that did not need to be spoken yet. He did not even know what they would be—what they *should* be. So as he didn't know what those words should be, he set them aside, sticking to words he knew he could say…wanted to say.

'It's a glorious morning,' he said. He paused. 'Let's just take things as they come.'

He'd said enough. He could see in her expression that she was glad of his words, for the sudden confusion and tension that had been there a moment earlier had ebbed away. In its place was a new expression, and one that caught at him.

Shyness.

As if finding herself in my bed is something she had not expected.

But then a rueful thought darted in him pointedly. There was a lot about Eliana that *he* had not expected.

He put it from him—he'd resolved not to go down that complex and confusing path. Not this morning…not this day.

He pulled the breakfast trolley against his side of the bed as he slid back in under the quilt, propping himself comfortably on his piled-up pillows.

'OJ to start with?' he asked, turning back to Eliana.

'Oh, yes—thank you,' she said.

She sounded a touch awkward, but he glossed it over. He didn't want her feeling awkward, or shy, or feeling anything other than that it was good to be sitting with him, side by side, on this glorious morning, with all of Paris awaiting them for the day.

He poured her a glass and handed it to her. Her fingers, he noticed, were careful not to touch his. He did not mind. It was not rejection, he knew, only self-conscious shyness.

A thought came to him, flickering in his mind.

That was the way she'd have been after our first night together, on our honeymoon…

Another thought, a realisation, came hard on its heels.

But this was our first night together...

It hung in his head for a moment—but there were too many other currents, too much confusion, too much shock circling around that truth and he would not deal with it. Not now. Not when he'd resolved, as he had just said to her, to take the day as it came. And right now it was coming with breakfast in bed, to be consumed enjoyably and leisurely.

Companionably.

That was what he felt, sitting back again with his own glass of orange juice. He let her be...let her get used to being here, like this, with him.

OJ consumed, he asked her what she might like to eat, then handed her a personal tray with croissants, butter pats and apricot jam, and a cup of coffee with hot milk. She placed it on her bedside table.

He got stuck in to his own breakfast—a more robust, seeded roll, with butter and a dollop of blackcurrant jam. He was hungry, and it went down quickly, and he reached for another.

At his side, Eliana was neatly getting through her croissant.

'You can't beat the French for breakfast in bed,' he said, helping himself to yet another roll. 'Though for a really substantial experience I'd always vote for a—what's that expression?—a full English. Bacon and eggs, smoked kippers, devilled kidneys—the works!' he said humorously.

He glanced at Eliana. She was more at ease now, he could tell, as if she was getting used to sitting here beside him. He wanted her to be at ease.

We're starting afresh.

The words were in his head and he knew them to be

true. Knew it with that same lightening of his spirit that had come as he had got out of bed, welcomed the new day, the new start.

What had gone before in their lives was still there—how could it not be? But last night had changed things. Though just how he still did not quite know for sure...

But he wasn't going to work that out now.

For now, he was going to do just what he'd said—take the day as it came.

For now, that was all he wanted.

Eliana sat back on the padded seat on the deck of the river cruiser. They were heading down the Seine to Giverny, to see Monet's famous gardens. The sun was warm on her, the breeze off the river as the cruiser gently made its way downstream pleasant on her face.

Outwardly, she and Leandros were spending the day much as they had the previous afternoon—sightseeing. And yet it felt fundamentally different. It *was* fundamentally different, she knew.

And it was not just because of what she had realised so undeniably the evening before, feeling Puccini's heartrending music pierce her own blind heart, piercing so much repression and denial, declaring to her the truth about herself and about why she had agreed to come here with Leandros.

Yes, that had changed her completely—she knew it and accepted it.

But it isn't just me who is changed.

Last night—as she had yielded willingly, wantonly, discovering in herself a passion and a sensuality to which she had given herself completely, knowing the truth about herself and accepting it, acknowledging it, instead of denying it and suppressing it—the revelation of her virginity had shocked Leandros to the core.

She bit her lip now, still troubled at how it had happened.

I didn't think he'd find out—I didn't realise just how... obvious...it would be!

Her marriage to Damian and the constrictions under which she had made it had no relevance to the truth she had faced up to as she'd sat in that *loge* at the opera and watched the two ill-fated lovers on the stage below, tormented and tormenting, destroying their own lives by the decisions they made. And yet, for all that, love had survived—even if the lovers themselves had not.

So it is with me.

She had given up on what she had once felt for Leandros six long years ago—buried it deep under the guilt she felt for what she had done. Yet it had survived despite what she'd done, despite the fateful decision she'd made all those years ago to abandon him, reject him.

Her eyes went to him now. He was standing a little way from her, but not far, leaning on the railing, looking out over the river at the passing scenery as Paris gave way to the countryside of Normandy. He looked relaxed, at ease, and she was glad—and grateful.

With feminine instinct and a little pang, she knew that his discovery that her marriage to Damian had been celibate had come as welcome news. That it had lessened, in some way, his sense of rejection by her when she had married Damian and not him.

Does he think it part of the retribution I deserved? To be denied a normal marriage with the husband I had chosen over him?

No—there had been no sense of that in him. And that

knowledge, that certainty that came from somewhere she knew not where, warmed her.

Her expression softened as her gaze fixed on him, the breeze ruffling his sable hair, the sleeves of his jumper pushed up to show his strong, tanned forearms as he leant against the railing. And the way he was being with her now warmed her too.

He'd been different from the moment she'd woken. Woken from that dream—the sweetest dream in all the world. A dream that had, as she'd woken, suddenly been no dream. Leandros truly had held her close, protected her, all night long...

Emotion welled in her, but there was sadness too. Sadness for all that might have been in her life. It pierced her now, the knowledge that however last evening and last night had changed things between them, it could never make right all that had gone wrong.

But for now, in this moment, this day, during this time with him, given to her as a blessing that she had never thought could be hers, what she had was enough.

'You can see why Monet loved his gardens so much,' Leandros said. 'Immortalising them in so many paintings.'

After the tour of Monet's house and gardens, he had repaired with Eliana for a late lunch in a nearby restaurant with a vine-covered terrace, busy with other visitors. The day was still warm enough to sit out, though he was glad of his lightweight sweater. Eliana wore a short-sleeved top with a matching bolero-style cardigan around her shoulders, paired with a flared skirt—all part of the wardrobe he'd supplied her with the previous day.

His gaze lingered—and yet it was not the gaze of the

previous day, veiled and assessing, holding at bay the part of his mind that was deploring the rashness of his decision to have anything to do with Eliana ever again, presenting her with an outward civility that masked the turbid, bitter emotions that warred with the driving desire for all that he sought only to sate and quench. To be free of for ever by indulging it. To taste and take the beauty that tormented him...

No, now it was less her beauty that held him—more her expression. He wanted to read it—be reassured by it.

'It was a good place to live out his life,' she answered now, her tone ruminative. 'There is always peace to be found in a garden.'

There was a softness in her eyes, as if she were thinking of more than Monet's garden.

'The garden at your father's villa was beautiful, as I remember,' he heard himself saying.

'Yes, it was always a comfort to him—as was the villa itself. He loved them dearly. I was always glad—'

She broke off, busying herself with breaking open her bread roll as they waited for their food to arrive.

'Glad?' he prompted.

She lifted her eyes and looked across at him. 'Glad he was able to end his days there.'

'Were you able to be with him?'

'Yes—Jonas granted me that, and I was grateful. After his stroke, my father...lingered...for two months. I stayed there for the duration.'

Leandros's eyes rested on her. There was a sadness in her face now, and he felt it pull at him.

'I...I heard that the villa will now pass to Damian's

cousin.' He felt uncomfortable saying it, but he did not mean it cruelly. Just the reverse.

Her marriage had not been easy. For whatever venal reason she'd made it, she had paid a high price for the rich living that was so important to her that she could not do without it.

She could not face poverty—even with me to share it with. She wanted what she was born to, and the threat of losing it made her reject me.

'Yes. Vassily will get it now—unless Jonas sells it, or pulls it down and replaces it with something modern, then sells that at a greater profit still. It's his business, after all, and how he made his money. Construction.'

'Or destruction,' Leandros riposted tightly. 'I only visited once, but it deserves keeping—whoever owns it.'

Leandros frowned again. Her father-in-law had driven a hard bargain when Eliana had married his son.

But it gave her what she wanted—she lived the high life with Damian.

Even if a celibate one…

A childless one.

He looked at her. 'Did you never think to give Jonas the grandchild he was set on? Even if Damian was gay, there was always the choice of conceiving through IVF and so on.'

She shook her head. 'Damian didn't want that,' she said.

She spoke calmly enough, but her expression was evasive. Leandros studied it.

'And you didn't want a child either?' he asked. 'A child would have ensured that you would still be part of Jonas's family now—he would not have cast you off as he has. Reduced you to the poverty I found you in.'

She didn't answer. The waitress came up with their dishes, placing them down in front of them, then heading off again. The moment passed, and Leandros let it. What point was there in probing Eliana's marriage? He would not disturb the day. There had been revelations enough last night—confusion and complexities. Today he wanted only ease and peace and Eliana at his side.

To pass the day as they were doing.

Companionably.

That word came again, just as it had come to him over breakfast, and then as they'd headed down river to take their leisurely, easy, peaceful cruise to Giverny, to explore the magical gardens of Monet's water lilies away from the cares and troubles of life, whether past or present.

He got stuck into his steak frites—simple, traditional French food—and washed it down with table wine, robust and drinkable. Eliana was eating fish, nothing delicate or sauced, but a grilled fillet of white fish, served with *pommes parmentier* and green beans.

He turned the conversation back to Monet, and to what they had seen.

'Though the water garden is extraordinary, and of course the famous Japanese-style bridge, and all the even more famous waterlilies, I don't like that it's separated from the house and the immediate garden of the house. Going through that linking tunnel was a disappointment.'

'Yes, I agree. It would be much better to have a house whose gardens encircled it—but then Monet had to buy what became the water garden from a neighbour, so I suppose that limited him.'

Leandros looked across at her. 'What kind of house and garden would you ideally like?'

The moment he spoke he regretted it. She would answer and say it was her father's villa, and that was lost to her.

Unless her next husband bought it back for her.

Next husband?

He had taunted her with being on the lookout for another rich husband to ensure she never had to face the poverty she'd always been determined not to experience—had bribed her, if it came to that, into agreeing to coming to Paris with him by saying he'd kit her out with a wardrobe suitable for ensnaring another rich husband—or even merely a rich lover.

And I'd move on once I had done with her.

He felt his jaw clench. Had he really thought that? Said that? Taunted her with it?

And I taunted her last evening, calling her Manon for betraying and rejecting a poor lover for a rich protector.

No—he would not go down that path again. Not now—not today.

Things had changed between them. Just how he did not know, and he did not want to. Not right now. Not today.

Nor the next day either. Or the one after that.

For now...

Just take the day as it comes.

And he knew—as he had known that morning, and knew now as he sat here with her, companionably, over lunch at this simple restaurant, eating a simple meal, having wandered in the gardens at Monet's house, with the afternoon and the rest of the day before them—that it was enough.

Eliana set her knife and fork down on the plate, feeling replete, reaching for her glass of wine. Dappled sunshine shone through the vines shading the terraced seating area and played on her face. Her mood was strange—yet peaceful. Despite Leandros asking her those questions.

Had she wanted to answer them?

All but one.

And that she had avoided. Must avoid. He would not be interested anyway, so what did it matter?

That he was asking questions at all was...was what? Curious? Surprising? Unexpected? Perhaps predictable. The revelation last night of how her marriage to Damian had not been what he'd assumed invited questions.

Not that her answers to any of them mattered—any more than why she and Damian had never tried to have a child.

None of it matters, because no answer I give can ever justify what I did to Leandros.

That was all there was to it—all the truth that it was necessary for her to face.

And the truth she had discovered last evening.

Her eyes went to him now, softening as they did so, and emotion flowed within her, strong and irrefutable. That was all that mattered to her now as she sat here with him, in this time she had.

It would not last. How could it? He had brought her here to free himself of her, purge himself of her, to take from her all that was left of what he'd once wanted.

And I will give it to him—freely and willingly. Even if it is all he wants of me, it is his...

Last night—and the debacle that had ended it—had merely been a...a delay...that was all. Now, tonight, she would be different—fulfilled.

All that he wants—and all that I want to give.

She felt that precious emotion flow again within her, warming her and comforting her. She would pay a price for it—as she had six years ago—but for now, *this* now, it would be her joy and her gift to him. And now she knew, with that certainty that had filled her since the discovery of the truth about why she had come to Paris with Leandros, that it was a gift to herself too.

'Shall we eat in tonight?'

Leandros's enquiry was tentative as they made their way back into their hotel. She might prefer to go out—see and be seen. If so, he would oblige. He was being…considerate. That was the word that came to him. Going easy on her, as he had all day, because—

Well, because. That was all. Still taking the day as it came. *And it's been good today.*

The river cruise, the gentle ambling around Monet's gardens, a leisurely lunch, some more ambling around the village of Giverny itself, then back to the river to glide serenely back upstream to Paris, looking out over the riverbanks that another painter, Seurat, had made equally as famous as Monet's waterlilies, with his river-bathing youths and his bourgeois promenaders along La Grande Jatte, immortalised in his trademark *pointilliste* style.

They had discussed it amiably, agreeing to differ— Eliana preferring the beauty of Monet, he the technical brilliance of Seurat.

We used to agree to differ all the time…

Even with her sheltered upbringing—or was it because of it, perhaps?—Eliana had been happy to disagree with him. It had been a novelty for him— the females he'd favoured had tended to agree with him. Too eagerly.

I called Eliana naive, overprotected by her doting father. But was I, in turn, spoilt by my looks and my wealth?

Did I take it for granted that I could always have what I wanted? Feel entitled to it?

It was a disquieting thought. If it were true, then had it only exacerbated the blow of Eliana's rejection of him? And besides...

I knew my father was only testing her, warning her he would disinherit me if I married her. I knew he only wanted her to prove her love for me—get her to marry me even with the threat of disinheritance and then relent. He would never have gone through with it. Would even have bailed out her father.

But Eliana had not known that. Had only known that if she went through with marrying him there would be no money—no money to keep her in the lifestyle she was used to, which she could not face losing when her father ran out of money.

So she had chosen Damian instead—and lived to see her father die, and all that he possessed pass to her father-in-law. Lived to face the very poverty she had married to avoid.

Come full circle.

Karma? Was that the word for it?

What we flee from we must eventually face?

The door to the elevator was slicing open, cutting off his thoughts. He was glad. He wanted to go back to his mandate for the day—to take things as they came.

And that included Eliana's preference for dinner.

She glanced at him as they entered the Résidence.

'That would be good...eating in,' she said.

'I think so too,' he affirmed. 'How about some coffee now?'

'I'd prefer tea,' she answered. 'But let me make it—and your coffee. Silly to summon the butler.'

She headed for the kitchen and Leandros followed her, discovering that a platter of fresh *patisserie* had been left for them. It looked good, and lunch had been a while ago now. He lifted a cherry, succulent and inviting, from the top of one of the mouth-watering selections, and realised that Eliana, kettle in hand, was looking at him, her expression strange.

'You used to pick the nuts off the baklava,' she said. 'Even though they were tiny and covered in syrup.'

'So I did,' he recalled. He'd forgotten. 'Then you'd dampen your serviette with water from your glass and hand it to me to wipe my sticky fingers...'

So long ago...so slight a gesture...so slight a memory.

And yet—

He put it from him. It was the present he was dealing with. And one issue in particular.

'I was thinking,' he said, 'whether you'd like another bath.'

She looked at him blankly.

He busied himself with the coffee machine, selecting his choice.

'After last night,' he said. 'In case—well, in case...'

He looked up, straight at her. He must say what he wanted to say. Needed to say.

'Last night...it changes things. So I want you to know—' He broke off. Then made himself go on. 'I expect nothing now, Eliana. Not any more.'

Where that had come from he didn't know. Knew only that he had needed to say it. That, in the end, was that what this day had been about—separating what had been before from what now was.

He was looking at her still. He could not read her face, nor her stillness. He went on speaking.

'So we'll just go on taking things as they come, OK? We can be as…as we are now. We can go on with our visit to Paris. Or…' he took a breath '…I can take you back to Thessaloniki, if that is what you prefer. It's…it's your call.' A thought struck him. 'Everything I bought you yesterday— all the clothes—obviously you will take them with you. That goes without saying. Anyway,' he carried on, wanting her to understand, 'for this evening, at least, let's just do what we agreed—eat in, take it easy…whatever.'

He paused again. She was still looking at him, her expression still unreadable. He needed a way out of there, so he took it, lifting up the platter of *patisserie*.

'I'll take these through,' he said, and got out.

Not knowing if he felt relief or its very opposite.

Or both.

Or why.

Eliana deposited her tea and Leandros's coffee on the low table by the sofa. Leandros was at one end, and he switched on the TV to an English language news channel. Her mind was still processing what Leandros had just said to her. She busied herself pouring milk into her tea, and Leandros did likewise for his coffee, then pushed the platter of *patisserie* towards her.

She selected one of the enticing-looking confections, depositing it on one of the two small plates she'd brought through for that purpose, handing the other plate to Leandros so he could make his selection. A small gesture…an intimate one.

A domestic one.

As if—

No—there was no 'as if' about it. She hadn't married him, she had never been his wife, and she never would be. Whatever was happening now had no domesticity to it at all.

Does he really want me to go back to Thessaloniki? Does he regret bringing me here?

She didn't know and couldn't tell. Knew only, with a clutch of emotion that she kept tight within her, what it was that *she* wanted.

In this sea of past bitterness and present doubt, of that she was sure.

I don't want to leave him—whatever he might want of me here, and however briefly. While he wants anything of me at all, I don't want to leave him.

Because this time, she knew, was all she would have—all she could ever have—of the man she had once loved and knew she still did.

CHAPTER TEN

LEANDROS STOOD BY the open windows giving out on to their Juliet balcony. The early-evening twilight was gathering. Gently, he eased the cork of the champagne bottle and it gave with a soft pop. As it did so, he heard the door of Eliana's bedroom open, and she emerged.

After tea and coffee she'd gone off to take another soothing bath, and he'd been glad, repairing to take a shower himself, and change into more relaxed clothes—a lightweight fine cashmere sweater over an open-necked shirt with turned-back cuffs. He'd touched base with his office while he had the opportunity. He'd left matters in good order, and they still were. He was glad of it. He didn't want distractions. Not now. Right now he had only one focus.

And she was standing right there.

She was hesitant, he could see, and he wanted that dispelled.

He made his smile warm, his voice warmer. 'Ah, there you are—how are you feeling?' There was genuine concern in his voice.

She didn't answer him directly. 'I soaked for ages—it was a real indulgence,' she said lightly. 'My apartment only has a shower, and the water is very seldom hot anyway.'

'Then have a bath every day!' he said, keeping his tone

as light as hers. He picked up an empty flute. 'Champagne? Or something different? Another G and T?'

Even as he asked her, his eyes were drinking her in. She'd put on one of her new dresses, softly draped in sage-green, halfway between dressy and casual—just right for dining in. She'd drawn her hair back into a low, loose chignon at the nape of her neck. He fancied she'd put on a little mascara, and maybe some lip sheen—just a very light touch of make-up to enhance her features. Whatever she'd done, with the dress and the hair and her own beauty she looked effortlessly lovely...

Something moved inside him as he looked at her—part of this strange new feeling he had about her that he knew was changing everything, even if he still did not understand how...

She stepped forward. 'Thank you—champagne would be very nice.'

She was still a little hesitant, and Leandros found himself wanting her to relax more. He wanted that sense of simply taking the day as it came to continue—without the complications, the confusion, the complexities that lay between them.

He filled her flute, and then his own, holding hers out to her.

She took it, murmuring her thanks.

'*Santé*,' he said in the same light tone. And as he did, he recalled the toast he'd so acerbically given the previous evening at the opera—'*My very own Manon.*'

It had been designed to taunt.

To mock.

To wound.

Regret, or something like it, smote him. Reappraisal—

maybe that was the right word? There was a reappraisal he should apply—one that she deserved.

Maybe I was being unfair—oh, not in saying that she only wanted to marry for money, but knowing that, having done so, she paid a price for it. A heavy price. To be unjustly accused by her domineering father-in-law of failing to give him the grandson he demanded when that was entirely because her marriage was celibate because her husband was gay! And then her father-in-law punished her by reducing her to poverty in her widowhood.

His thoughts were sober.

Maybe she did not deserve any more retribution from me for what she did.

Maybe retribution—if that was even the right word now—had already been exacted from her...

Maybe she had already paid her price for her faithlessness.

And maybe, therefore—the words from that morning came again into his head—*we should start over.*

They'd made a start—today had been a good day, a much easier, more peaceable day, without their previous guarded, superficial civility. He had the grace to acknowledge that the bitterness he harboured was as deep within him as it had ever been, while she'd kept to an air of passive detachment. But today had not been like that. It had been—

Companionable.

There was that word again—the one that kept coming to him.

Almost like we used to be.

The thought flickered in his head like a light that might or might not dispel the shadows.

'*Santé,*' she echoed, dipping her head to take a taste of the gently beading champagne.

'I've taken the liberty of ordering dinner for us,' he said. 'I hope you don't mind.'

He told her the choices he'd made, saying there was still time to change them, but she shook her head.

'It all sounds delicious,' she said. 'Thank you. And thank you, too, for taking me to Giverny today.'

He glanced at her. 'You don't have to thank me,' he said. 'It's all part of…'

He stopped. Part of what? Part of what he was offering her because of what he was getting in return? Like the clothes he'd bought her? This stay in a luxury hotel?

Put like that, he didn't like the implication. Which didn't make sense. It hadn't troubled him when he'd put it to her in Thessaloniki over dinner. Outlining what he was offering her—what she would get out of it in return.

'Yes,' he heard her say quietly, acceptingly, 'I know. But thank you all the same—for dinner tonight, and last night, and taking me to the opera, and to Giverny today, and Notre Dame and Sainte-Chapelle yesterday.'

He shook his head in negation. 'I didn't mean it like that.' He paused. 'I don't want it to be like that.'

He had wanted it—but not any more. Now he knew he no longer simply wanted her gratitude for bringing her to Paris—and the reason he had brought her here.

For sex—that's what you brought her here for. You spelt it out plainly enough.

Yet somehow, right now, it was an uncomfortable thought. He felt his mind sheer away. And not just because there was suddenly a sordid edge to it…to what he'd offered her.

Because even if she's only accepted to get out of that wretched dump she has to live in and get her hands on a decent wardrobe again, so she can kickstart her way back into a luxe lifestyle, that doesn't justify my offer. Because what does it say about me that I made such an offer? Doesn't it just reduce me to her level?

His mouth twisted. Well, right now there wasn't much likelihood of his making good on the reason he'd brought her to Paris. Not after last night. And it wasn't just a question of enough soothing baths...

He'd hurt her physically. He hadn't meant to—hadn't even known he could, in that way—but that didn't change the fact that he had done so.

'I think,' he said haltingly, knowing this was something he wanted to make clear to her, and finding the resolve to do it, 'that from now...well, separate bedrooms.'

As he said it, there was instant conflict in his head. He'd said the right thing, the decent thing. But the moment he'd done so scorching memory had come—vivid...leaping into punishing hyper-consciousness...

She'd torn herself away from him, in his bed, almost at the very consummation of the inferno that had been consuming him—consuming her too. For she had lit that inferno by coming to him as she had, and he had gone up in flames, and so had she, with mutual desire burning them with the white heat of passion unleashed.

But from the moment of her shocking revelation to this moment now he'd assiduously, doggedly, refused to let into his head what had come before. Yet now it seared white-hot.

Gliding up to me, hair loose and wanton, body sensuous and irresistible to me, winding her arms around me, reaching for my mouth with hers...

He had been lost instantly, totally. That had been no self-sacrificing abasement, no offering herself to him as some kind of atonement. That had been Eliana just as he'd said he'd wanted her to be—eager, aroused, passionate. And he had been likewise. Instantly. Consumingly...

He slammed down hard on the memory. It was the situation now he was dealing with. A situation that made any repetition of what had happened last night completely out of the question.

'So you can be comfortable,' he said now.

She was looking at him questioningly, uncertainly. 'Leandros, why...why are you being so nice to me?'

He frowned. 'I'd be a brute not to be, in the circumstances. It appals me that I hurt you—'

She shook her head. 'I don't just mean separate bedrooms. I mean...well, all day today. And...and last night too. Making hot milk for me...all that... And you're being nice to me now too.'

He took a mouthful of champagne. Her question had been direct—his answer was not.

'Why shouldn't I be?' he countered.

Her frown remained. 'Because you hate me,' she said.

He stilled. '*Hate* you?' His voice was hollow.

'I don't blame you for that—I have no right to do so.' She spoke as if she had not heard him. 'But...' She took a breath and he realised she was not as calm as she was appearing. 'But even though you discovered that my marriage was not...not what the world thought it was...not in that way...that doesn't change anything between us, does it?'

He didn't answer, only lifted his champagne flute to his mouth, taking another slow mouthful, as if to give himself time, then lowering it again.

His expression changed, and he looked directly at her.

'Eliana, even if…even if you went into your marriage with Damian open-eyed about his sexual orientation—and I hope that you did…that you knew what you were letting yourself in for—do you…do you ever regret it? Regret marrying him instead of me?'

He had said it—asked the question that he had never allowed himself to ask before. For what purpose would there have been in her answer? Not while she was married to Damian certainly.

But if she had come to regret it she could have had the marriage annulled for non-consummation…or just gone for a divorce—

'No.'

Her one-word answer was quietly spoken, but there was in it something that made Leandros know she had spoken only the truth.

'No, I don't regret marrying Damian. It was my choice to do so—and it would be my choice again.'

Leandros felt a heaviness inside him at her answer. He pursued it to its conclusion—the conclusion he already knew…had known for six long years. Now stated again.

'Because if you'd married me you'd have faced poverty—and you couldn't face that.'

'No.'

Again, the one-word answer gave tacit agreement to what he had said, and was quietly spoken, but it was neither hesitant, nor holding regret.

'I could not have faced the consequences of marrying you. And so for that reason, whatever kind of marriage I had with Damian, I cannot—*do* not—regret it.'

Her expression changed.

'It's the only truthful answer I can give. I'm… I'm sorry I can't give you any other. And I'm sorry that I hurt you… that I killed the love you felt for me.' She took a breath. 'And I am glad, for your sake, that you no longer feel anything for me—'

She broke off, looked away, out of the window, over the rooftops of Paris.

There had been a bleakness in her voice just then that had been absent from the quiet, unhesitant way she'd told him she did not regret her marriage to Damian. But it was her last words that echoed inside Leandros's head. They were true—of course they were true. How could they be anything other than true?

And yet—

Are they still true? Do I feel nothing for her?

The question hung in his consciousness, wanting an answer—an answer he could not give.

For a moment he stood still, eyes resting on her averted face, on her fingers curved around the stem of the champagne flute she was holding. Then slowly, so very slowly, his hand reached out to touch the curve of her wrist…so lightly…so fleetingly.

'Things change, Eliana,' he said softly. 'They've changed already between us. They could change again.'

He let his hand fall away. He was conscious of the beat of his own heart. The silence between them. She did not turn back, so he could not see her face, but he saw her fingertips around the stem of her glass tighten. And her free hand moved to fold over the place where he had touched her so briefly—so gently.

Was she sheltering herself against his touch? Or sheltering the touch itself? How could he tell? How could he know?

How can I know anything about her, about what she feels? And why should I care?

He did not know that either. Knew only that somehow, now, he did care.

His own words to her echoed.

'Things change, Eliana. They've changed already between us. They could change again.'

Could they? Could they change again?

And do I want them to?

That was another unanswered question. So many unanswered questions...

So much confusion and complexity—how can I make sense of it all?

The sound of the doorbell was intrusive in the silence that had fallen between them. Was it welcome? Or the opposite? Whichever it was, he turned back into the room, pulling open the door to admit the butler and his minions.

The arrival of dinner needed to be attended to, and maybe he was glad of it. That exchange with Eliana had been too intense, going too deep into past and present. He needed respite from it—and maybe so did she.

She seemed glad to take her place at the table in their dining room while a resplendent meal was presented to them.

Leandros had specifically selected a menu that would enable their entrée—*boeuf bourguignon*—to be kept warm in chafing dishes, with chilled *tarte au citron* for dessert, so that he could dismiss the staff...not have them hover.

Yet the moment they were gone he felt silence threaten again. He dismissed it with resolve. He'd wanted an easier day, and wading into asking questions such as he had on the balcony was not conducive to that end. Now he wanted that sense of ease back again. Wanted the atmosphere lightened.

Wanted to feel again what he had felt during the day.

Companionable.

Deliberately, he raised his refilled champagne glass to Eliana across the table.

'Bon appetit,' he said. 'I hope our dinner is as delicious as you have said it sounds.'

He made his voice light, replacing his flute and picking up his fork to start to do justice to the beautifully layered vegetable terrine that was their first course.

'I'm not sure what all the layers are,' he pondered, 'except that one of them, judging by its colour, is definitely beetroot.'

'There's courgette in there somewhere,' Eliana answered, and he was glad that her tone of voice was as light as his. 'And perhaps asparagus?'

They went on identifying the multi-coloured, multi-textured layers. It was easy conversation, light and inconsequential. But it served its purpose. Lightened the atmosphere.

He glanced towards her. As ever, her beauty made his breath catch.

It comes to her naturally—she makes no effort, but it is there all the time.

Memory came—how struck he'd been when he'd first been courting her, wooing her, making her his own, by just how naturally beautiful she was. Unsophisticated, yes, unlike the females he usually ran with, but her beauty had been in her smile, her eyes, her sun-kissed hair... In the way she'd laughed, and dropped her gaze when he looked at her—not in a flirtatious way, or to entice him... Although sometimes he would catch her stealing a look at him from beneath her smoky lashes...a look of longing...

He'd liked that—had liked to bring the colour flushing to her soft cheeks when he'd paid her compliments, which she'd absorbed like a flower drinking in the warming rays of the sun...

I thought I'd found a woman different from any that I had known. One to fall in love with.

He hadn't intended to fall in love at all. It had not been on his agenda—but Eliana had changed all that. With her in his life he'd no longer wanted to play the field, hadn't been interested in the chic, sophisticated females he'd once focussed his attentions on. Eliana had swept him away— swept him totally away.

Until she'd walked away from him. Handed back his ring. Walked out of his life.

But now she's back in it. I've let her in. Thinking I knew why.

His gaze rested on her now, and he felt again the confusion he'd felt in the night, when he'd realised the truth about her marriage...felt again, even more intensely, what had passed between them out on the balcony just now.

What do I want of her? What do I want at all?

No answers came—or only one, to which he now returned.

He wanted to be with her as he had been today—easy, peaceable...companionable.

Nothing more than that.

Nothing less.

CHAPTER ELEVEN

THE WALL-HUNG TV blazed with a last burst of colour and declared *The End*. Robin Hood and his Maid Marian had just ridden off into their personal sunset. The choice of film had been mutual, and just right. A colourful swashbuckler, traditional Hollywood, as familiar as it was enjoyable.

Eliana stretched her legs from being curled up under her on the sofa. Beside her, but not too close, Leandros sat lounging back, long legs extended, crossed at the ankles, picking at the last of the *petits fours* on the coffee table.

He turned towards her.

Smilingly.

'Daft, but fun,' he said.

She gave a light laugh. 'Definitely,' she agreed.

Her gaze lingered on him a moment, eyes veiled, as if she was self-conscious suddenly, and then she reached for her wine glass. They had eaten a leisurely dinner, and had been finishing off the luscious dessert wine since they'd repaired to the sofa. The mood that had prevailed since their outing to Giverny still held, and Eliana was glad of it. Yet a sadness of sorts plucked at her. Leandros had wanted a different answer to the question he had put to her. Different from the one she had given him: that she would make the same choice again as she had six years ago.

I can't undo the past.

His voice echoed in her head. *'Things change, Eliana.'*

But the past did not change. What had been true then was still true. And her feelings too. Feelings she could never smother or deny, though they would only bring her yet more heartache in the end.

So be content with this—with what is here and now.

'Fancy watching anything else?' Leandros asked in an easy tone.

She gave a shake of her head, finishing the last of her sweet wine and getting to her feet.

'Time for bed,' she said lightly.

Did something flicker in his eyes? If it did, she discounted it. 'Separate bedrooms' he had said, and she knew he had said it out of concern for her, after the debacle of the night before. But that would not be. That would not be at all.

She gave a secret smile, but poignant. The past was gone. The future was impossible. Only the present was hers.

And that was what she would claim and give to him.

Give to us both.

And she would hold it in her heart against the long, empty years ahead, when Paris was over and done with and this precious time with Leandros would be nothing more than a memory...

Leandros clicked off the TV, his gaze following Eliana as she retreated to her bedroom. He did not want her to do so, but he had given his word.

Memory came. Tormentingly. He sought to hold it back. He would not—*must* not—recall the night before...recall the feel of her naked body beneath his, her eager mouth, the sensual white-out of his instantly inflamed passion, his desire…

The bedroom door shut behind her, and he got to his feet. Sitting beside her as they'd watched the ancient Hollywood film had been both good…and bad. Good to be so close to her—bad to be so close to her. She'd sat curled up, relaxed, her hair falling from its chignon, the soft drape of her dress shaping her breasts…

It had been hard to focus on the swashbuckling going on onscreen. Hard to think of her now, in her bedroom, removing her dress, loosening her hair…

He snatched up the coffee tray and the wine glasses, taking them through into the kitchen. Busying himself, he washed them up to give him something to do—something to stop him thinking about the rashness of promising Eliana 'separate bedrooms', even though that had been the only decent thing to do after the debacle of the previous night.

Leaving the cups and glasses on the draining board, he headed to his own room. He would take a shower—tonight he definitely would.

He did so, turning the temperature as low as was necessary—which was very low. He endured it as much as he could—it was a cure, but a punishing one. He stepped out of the cubicle, seized a towel, wrapping it around his hips, grateful for its warmth. He grabbed another one, patting his chest and shoulders dry, then reached for his toothbrush.

As he brushed his teeth he felt the same heaviness fill him that had assailed him on the balcony, when she'd told him what he knew with bitter truth he had wanted her not to say.

I wanted her to say she regretted marrying as she did…

regretted rejecting me as she did. That she would never do so given a second chance. I wanted her to tell me that if she got that second chance she would choose me this time...

But she had said none of that.

He frowned at his own reflection. His jawline was darkening, his hair damp from the shower. His gaze at himself was interrogating.

But that was the past—and it is the present we have now.

His own words sounded again in his head. *'Things change—they can change again.'*

Could they?

And would I want them to?

And Eliana? Would she want them to? Last night she had come to him, just as he had told her he wanted her to, in passion and desire, answering his for her. Last night he had thought that enough—thought it all that he wanted of her. But now...?

His promise to her of 'separate bedrooms', of making no more demands of her, setting no expectations on her, had negated the very reason he had brought her here to Paris with him. Negated hers for being here.

It was a promise he would honour. But tonight, he knew, as he replaced his toothbrush, would be an ordeal.

For himself.

Heaviness still weighing him down, he cut the light above the sink, saw his bleak reflection vanish, and went back out into his bedroom.

Where Eliana was waiting for him in his bed.

She saw him stop short. Sudden doubt assailed her, then vanished. She lifted her hand to him. Her other hand was holding the quilt across her breasts. Her hair was loose on her bare shoulders.

She said his name. Her voice low and tender.

For a moment he did not move.

And then—

He was there, taking her hand, pressing it tight, coming down to sit beside her, his eyes pouring into hers. They were alight with urgency—and with doubt. Searching for her meaning.

'Is this what you want? Eliana—tell me. It must be what you want—only what you want. Or—'

She did not let him finish. His low, husky voice had been fraught, questioning. She lifted her other hand, placed a finger across his mouth. The movement made the quilt slip, exposing one breast, but she did not mind. How could she? She was here for him—and for herself.

For us both.

Her eyelids dipped and she raised her mouth to his, the hand that had touched his now cupping his cheek. It was rough to the touch, but she did not mind that either, smiled at it as she kissed him.

Not urgently, or on fire, but sweetly, softly—tenderly.

She drew back, her hand in his, pressing him back. She held his gaze again.

'This is our time, Leandros.' Her voice was soft and low and very, very certain. 'This time is ours…'

Again, for a moment he did not speak—not with his voice. But with his eyes… She felt her breath catch. Oh, with his eyes he said all that she wanted to hear.

'Eliana…' He breathed her name, and it seemed to her a blessing and a gift.

A redemption for all that she had done to him and the

pain she had caused—to him, and to herself. She did not ask for forgiveness, only for this. For this coming together now, as they would have done so long ago.

This is our wedding night.

The words were in her head, and it seemed they were a gift and a blessing too.

And then there were no more words, only the sweetness of his kiss and all that came thereafter, as gently, tenderly, he lay her back and finally made her his own.

She was softness, she was sweetness, she was wonder. And a delight to savour and behold…to tenderly caress and to possess. But unhurriedly and carefully…oh, so carefully. The flame between them was a gentle one, a slow-burning one, taking its time. For why should there be a rush? They had all night.

He had one focus only: that *this* time he would make amends. Last night there had been a desperate hunger, an urgency to assuage his needs and hers. Tonight he would be as gentle, as patient, as she desired—as he desired too. And with each trace of his lips, of his fingertips, with the smoothing of her sweet delights with his palms, from breasts to thighs, and all that lay between, he would give her the slow, sensuous pleasure that he was receiving from her in return.

This was passion—oh, this was passion, indeed. But slowed to a tempo that Leandros knew with every instinct he possessed was what this moment needed. What Eliana needed.

And what I need too.

Time—just time. So simple and so precious. As precious as the little sighs of pleasure that sounded in her throat as he drew from her, slowly and sensuously, the delight that he knew he could give her, felt her own body's response to his. Slowly and sensuously, he took her on that journey with each soft kiss, each languorous caress, taking his time, cupping her breasts that swelled to his touch, trailing his fingertips along the silken columns of her thighs, the delicate folds, drawing from her yet more low sighs of soft, melting pleasure.

She wound her arms loosely around his neck, gazing up at him. There was ardency in her gaze, invitation in her smile. And when he moved his body over hers that invitation was in her body too. Slowly, with infinite care, infinite patience, he eased into her, pausing, as his lips moved across hers tenderly and reassuringly, to let her body accommodate him.

He heard her sigh—with completion, with acceptance. Felt her enclose him, hold him, fold around him. Bring him to his own moment...

He lifted his mouth from hers. 'Eliana, I can't— I can't... hold back...'

Though he had known he must be infinitely gentle, now it was impossible to deny his body the fulfilment it sought when it had found so perfect a union with her, so absolute a fusion.

Her hands cradled the nape of his neck and she smiled at him.

'No more can I,' she said, and as if a bow had been released she arched her spine, her fingers flexed into his nape. Her head was going back. Face transformed.

She cried out—but not with pain. Never that—never again. With an ecstasy that pierced him to the core he felt her convulse around him, and in that moment came his.

Fusion upon fusion, they held each other as their flesh became one. As they became one…

Eliana lay in Leandros's arms. It was the sweetest place to be in all the world. Her hand was splayed upon his chest, the other wound around his waist. Their thighs mingled, tangled. His arm curved along her spine, holding her close to him, his other cradled her head against his shoulder.

They did not speak. There was no need to. No need for words. Only for this moment, this time, held in each other's arms in the velvet darkness of the night.

So much filled her. So much she could not believe her heart could hold it all. It flowed from her, enveloping him, encompassing him, binding him to her.

For this moment. For this time. For now.

This now was everything to her. All the world and more.

She was in the arms of the man she loved.

But she must lose him again.

A cry of protest rose within her, silent and imploring.

But not yet—not yet. Grant me this time—this precious time—before I must break my heart again.

She had been granted time. That much had been given to her.

A week.

A week in which to live out a lifetime of her love for him.

'Time for our treats,' announced Leandros. 'Lunch was a long time ago!' He pointed to a nearby bench. 'What about that spot?'

'Perfect,' said Eliana. She looked around as they headed for the bench. 'I had no idea the Luxembourg gardens were so vast!' she exclaimed.

Everywhere there were vistas, a mix of formal gardens and more natural—even an orchard.

'Over sixteen hectares,' answered Leandros, quoting from the tourist guide.

They settled down on the bench at the edge of the gravelled pathway. Across the gardens they could hear the happy laughter and glee of children enjoying the rides and slides, and from their bench they could see the huge stone pond, where toy boats were being sailed.

Leandros undid the ribbons around the box of *patisserie* he'd been carefully carrying since they'd availed themselves of a convenient *boulangerie* after lunch. The good weather was holding, and he was glad, but autumn was on the way. The sun was not as warm, and the leaves of the trees in the gardens were visibly beginning to turn.

But for now it was pleasant—very pleasant indeed—to sit here, legs outstretched, crossed at the ankles, his feet in comfortable trainers for all the walking he and Eliana were doing as they made their daily explorations of the city.

Contentment filled him. How could it not?

He smiled at Eliana. She was wearing lightweight trousers in dark blue, and a lightweight knit with a vee neck that showed off the delicate sculpture of her neck. Her hair was caught back with a barrette, her make-up only lip gloss and mascara. Yet his breath caught at her beauty.

With so much more than her beauty.

She was leaning forward, lifting the lid of the cardboard box holding the *patisserie*.

'The *religieuse* for me,' she said decisively, helping herself to the choux and crème confection, sinking her teeth into it as she sat back to enjoy what France was so famous for.

'I'll take the *mille-feuille*,' Leandros said, and did so.

They consumed their indulgences companionably. But then they did everything companionably. And so much more than merely companionably...

As if the last six years had never been. As if this truly were our honeymoon—the one we should have had together.

Shadows flickered in his eyes.

But she hadn't wanted that—hadn't wanted a honeymoon with him.

So why now? This time with me?

He could not think it was for the reason he'd first put to her. Not any longer. How could it be? She'd refused to let him buy any more clothes for her. Refused, even more tellingly, when he'd stopped outside a jeweller's and invited her to tell him what she liked best in the display.

'But I want to get you something—a souvenir from Paris,' he'd said.

She'd only shaken her head, then taken his hand to continue their walk.

They were doing a lot of walking, seeing all the sights, and he was delighting in showing them to her—from the Eiffel Tower to the Pantheon, from Napoleon's tomb to the Arc de Triomphe. They'd wandered through the Tuileries gardens and along the Champs-Elysées, strolled through the Latin Quarter, stopping for coffee at the cafés made famous by the French *philosophes* and intellectuals and artists, sampling the rich bounty of Paris's art galleries... There was so much to see...impossible to do it all in just one visit.

He'd said as much over dinner one evening, at the restaurant he'd taken her to—one of the most renowned in

Paris, to which she'd worn another of the evening gowns he'd chosen for her in a rich vermilion. It had taken his breath away when she'd emerged from her bedroom in all her splendour. The bedroom that was now really only her dressing room...serving no other purpose.

Because each night—each blissful night—she was his... completely his. Ardent and passionate, her desire matching his. Night after night.

'There is still so much to see,' he'd said to her that night across the candlelit table. 'Too much for a single visit.'

Had it been the candlelight flickering on her face that had made it look shadowed? She hadn't answered him, only smiled and praised the wine, lifted her glass.

He'd lifted his, and tilted it to her. 'To our next visit,' he had said.

Yet even as he'd said the words he'd wondered if he should. Wondered again now, as they emptied the box of *patisserie* between them.

This time with her—could it last? Should it last?

I wanted to bring her here to free myself of her.

Perhaps he should remember that...

He closed the empty box. The delights inside, those sweet indulgences, were all gone. Consumed.

Eliana was getting to her feet, dusting the crumbs off her.

'My fingers are all sticky. I need to rinse them in the pond.'

His were as well, and he followed her, depositing the empty box in a bin, its purpose served. The water in the pond was cool as he dabbled his fingers, shaking them dry.

'You used to pick the nuts off the baklava—'

Eliana's reminder plucked at him. That time with her

back then had been as sweet as this time now. But it had passed. This time would pass too.

Maybe I should just be content with what we have now and then let it go.

Just as he must let go the poisoned past between them, he must let Eliana go…slip out of his life.

He must move on from her.

But not quite yet.

He smiled as he looked down at her, perched on the stone edge of the pond, rinsing her fingers.

'How do you fancy seeing if we can hire a model yacht to race?' he invited.

Her answering laugh, and her smiling eyes meeting his, confirmed his thoughts.

No, not yet.

CHAPTER TWELVE

ELIANA'S PHONE WAS buzzing softly but insistently, waking her up. It was morning, but early still. As she groped for it the call went to voicemail—but the number was still displayed.

Immediately, she slid out of bed. Leandros was still asleep, and she was grateful. She hurried from the room, wanting the privacy of her own bedroom so she could hear the voicemail. But after she did, she set the phone down, sank down on the unused bed, consternation in her face.

Then, her breathing shallow and agitated, she got to her feet.

She needed to go—right now.

Leave Paris.

Leave Leandros.

Leave this brief happiness that had come so unexpectedly, had been so unlooked-for—which she had always known could only be brief and soon must end.

And now it had.

Leandros sat in his airline seat, his hands clenched over the armrests. His face was tight, expressionless. But behind the mask of his face a storm was taking place.

She had gone. Walked out on him. No explanation. No justification. No attempt at an excuse. Nothing.

Except a scrawled note.

Leandros, I have to get back to Thessaloniki.

The words stabbed in his head as the plane flew on above the clouds, heading south. Stabbed him—and mocked him. Just as the past had mocked him, was still mocking him now. It was happening again. She was walking out on him, walking away. Just as she had done before.

But this time—

Why? Why is she doing it again now? Six years ago she left me to marry money—but what is there for her in leaving me now? There is nothing for her in Thessaloniki—just the scraps from Jonas Makris's begrudging table!

He closed his eyes, his grip on the armrests of his seat tightening so that his knuckles were white with it. The rest of her words stabbed at him.

We knew from the start that Paris was only to set ourselves free from the past—nothing more.

Now the stab went deeper. Mocking him even more. Yes, his wanting to be free of her, to stop her haunting him, tormenting him, had been the reason he'd taken her to Paris. He'd wanted nothing else. But now—after those carefree, contented days with her, those incandescent nights with her...

Is that still what I want?

Her final words tolled in his head.

Nothing more.

His eyes flared open, bleak and empty. And those words tolled again.

Nothing more.
Each one was a stab to his throat.

Eliana was at the bank, her face set. She was going to have to raid her minuscule pot of savings, assiduously hoarded out of what had been left of her allowance and her earnings. With a grim expression, she made the payment she had gone there to make. Then headed back to her apartment. Not that she could afford to live even there now.

She felt a flicker of unease. What she was doing was risky—but she had no choice. Her finances demanded it.

Her mind flitted back, like a magnet seeking true north, to where it longed to go—where *she* longed to go. But that was barred to her now.

I took the 'now' that was offered to me knowing that it could not last. And now that 'now' is gone.

Regret mingled with guilt—a familiar toxic mix. But now it was not for the past of six years ago. It was for the past of only the day before yesterday. But there was nothing she could do about it. Only endure it. Endure it as she had before—six years ago and every year since then. And now once more.

This time it was more unbearable. More agonising.

To break her heart a second time...

The taxi pulled up outside the run-down apartment block and Leandros got out, his face set. Why had he come here? He should have stuck to writing Eliana out of his life—again. But after one sleepless night in Athens he had flown up to Thessaloniki.

Wanting answers.

She owes me that.

The words of the totally inadequate note she had left incised in his brain.

Why? Why did she have to come back? After what we had in Paris...

Someone was coming out of the block, and he used that opportunity to get into the shabby lobby. The elevator had a notice on it saying it was awaiting repairs—the same notice as last time—so he vaulted up the stairs, chipped and stained.

He gained Eliana's floor. Rapped on her door.

Demanding entrance.

Eliana paused frowningly in the act of closing her suitcase. The landlord's agent? Come to inspect the premises before she left?

She went to open the door, not wanting a confrontation, but steeling herself for one all the same.

It came—but not with the landlord's agent.

She gave a gasp.

Leandros strode in, turned. But not before he had seen the suitcase on her bed, the larger one already closed and standing by the door. He took in the stripped bed, the absence of any of her belongings. His eyes swept back to hers. Skewered them.

'Moving out?' he said.

His voice was calm, but it made a hollow inside her for all that.

He filled the room—filled so much more. She hung on to the door-jamb, just to give her strength. A strength that was ebbing away like ice on a hot stove, just as swiftly. Her mouth had dried, but she had to answer him.

'Yes,' she said.

His skewering gaze pinned her. The planes of his face were stark. Only once had she seem him thus—when she had slid his ring from his finger and walked out of his life.

'I…I have to go,' she said.

He frowned suddenly. 'You've been evicted?'

She shook her head. 'No… I'm just…just moving somewhere else.'

Weakness was flooding through her—and something quite different that had nothing to do with the dismay that was paralysing her. A longing so intense she felt faint with it. But it was a longing that had no place in her life.

'Where?' he demanded.

'Just…somewhere else.'

She knew there was evasion in her voice. He'd heard it, she could see. See it in the sudden icing of his gaze. The narrowing of his eyes. The starkness of his cheekbones.

'So tell me where.'

Her heart was thudding, her hand still splayed across the door-jamb, clinging to it for support.

'It doesn't matter where. Or why.'

He took a step towards her and she threw up a hand, as if to ward him off.

'Leandros, it doesn't *matter*! It doesn't matter where I'm going, or why. It isn't…it isn't anything to do with you.'

He stared at her. 'You say that to me,' he said slowly, 'after Paris?'

Her face contorted. 'Leandros—Paris was…was… Well, what it was…' How could she tell him what it had been to her? 'But it was never going to last—and you didn't want it to either.' She shut her eyes a moment, then sprang them open again. 'Oh, Leandros…' Her voice had changed… she heard anguish in it. 'I know why you took me there.

I know the memory of what I did to you six years ago has haunted you—poisoned you. At first I thought that I owed you Paris, and I was prepared to go through with it. But then… Well—' she drew a ragged breath '—things changed. Maybe…' she half lifted a hand towards him, then let it drop away '…even healed,' she said. 'Or…or something like that. Whatever it was, it was…good.' Her voice dropped. 'But it could never have lasted. It just couldn't.'

'Did you not want it to?'

His voice was hollow, as if something had been emptied out of it.

He stepped towards her. 'Eliana, what happened in Paris—it *was* good! You know it was good. We made it good. I said to you that we could change, and we did— both of us!' His voice was vehement—urgent. 'Why lose it? Why walk away from it?'

How could she answer? It was impossible.

She took another ragged breath. 'I wish you hadn't come here…chasing after me. There's no point.'

'So where are you going? Why? And why do you not answer what I've asked you?'

She could see a nerve working in his cheek, the starkness in his face as she stayed silent.

Then suddenly, he gave an oath, his expression changing completely. 'You're going to someone else—'

There was no emotion in his voice, yet it chilled her to the core. Chilled her—and handed her what she desperately, despairingly, needed.

'Yes,' she said.

For one unendurable moment his eyes held hers, and in them was what she had seen only once before, on that unbearable day she'd handed him back his ring. Then, without a word, he walked past her.

Out of the apartment.

Out of her life—a second time.

She closed her eyes, hearing his hard, heavy footsteps on the stairs heading down. As hard and heavy as the hammer-blows of her heart. Slaying her.

Leandros was in his office, but he was not working. Work was impossible, though it was piling up. Over and over in his head he could hear a replay of his last exchange with Eliana.

'You're going to someone else.'

And her one-word answer.

'Yes.'

One word—one single word—and it damned her. Damned her to hell. But he didn't want her in hell. Hell was where *he* was—and seeing her again would be another circle of hell for him, another agony.

How could she be going to someone else? *How* could she be leaving him? After what they'd had in Paris?

After what we claimed for ourselves.

'Healing', she'd called it, and the word blazed in his head now. Yes, that was exactly, totally what it had been. He felt it now, the truth of it filling him.

I found her again—the woman I once loved.

But now he had lost her again.

Rebellion rose up in him.

Six years ago I let her leave me. I let money be more important to her than loving me. I let her do that. I didn't challenge it... I didn't fight her for it.

Because six years ago she hadn't been worth fighting for.

But this time…

This time she is.

Whatever had happened to her in the dysfunctional marriage she'd made, she had changed. She must have changed. Or else why would she not have taken from him everything she could? All that he had originally promised her? She'd refused gifts of jewellery, left her couture wardrobe behind. Walked away with nothing of what he'd offered her when he'd told her he wanted her to go to Paris with him.

And what they'd had in Paris had been *good*.

Maybe I didn't understand what was happening to me— to us. Maybe I still wasn't sure what I wanted. But now— Now I won't lose it. I won't let it go, never to return.

He felt his hands clench into fists. *This* time he would not give up on her.

He stared, unseeing, across his office. Emotion was churning inside him. Powerful. Insistent. Focussed on one goal only.

Eliana.

Getting her back.

Eliana was back at work, back to stacking shelves, back at the till, back to fetching and carrying. She wasn't working full-time any longer, but the wage she earned was still essential to her finances. The supermarket was farther away from where she was now based, and she was on the lookout for something closer. She wished she could find something better paid, but that was unlikely, given her lack of marketable skills.

She gave a sigh. No point wanting things that were impossible.

Like wanting Leandros.

No, she mustn't let her thoughts go there, or her memories. It was like pouring acid on an open wound.

I survived a broken heart six years ago—I can survive it again. I must.

Because there was no alternative. As before, she'd made her choice—and now she was living with it.

No point complaining or repining.

Numbly, mechanically, she went on stacking shelves.

Leandros frowned. This apartment block might be in a better street than the dump Eliana had lived in before, and it was in better condition—cleaner and well-kept—but it was not what he'd expected. Had she really taken up with someone who lived here?

But it was not where that someone lived that he cared about—it was that there was a 'someone else' at all.

How could she? How could she after what we had in Paris? Did it mean nothing to her?

His thoughts darkened as he walked into the lobby. Six years ago her time with him had meant nothing to her either...

He gave her name to the concierge—at least this block had one. The man frowned for a moment, then his face cleared.

'Second floor, apartment six—opposite the stairwell,' he said. 'Do you want me to phone?'

Leandros shook his head, vaulting up the stairs.

As he gained her floor he stopped dead. *What the hell was he doing?* He'd trekked here to fight for her—thinking that *this* time she was worth fighting for. But was he just fooling himself? Whatever had happened in Paris, she had still walked away from him as she had done before.

Six years ago he'd known who she'd left him for. And why.

Last time around I knew. This time around I don't need to.

Could not bear to.

That was the sorry truth of it.

He made to turn away. He could not face this. Could not bear it. Whatever she was doing in a place like this, whoever she was with, he didn't want to know.

She's gone—and I've lost her. Lost her just as I lost her before. I have to accept it.

He twisted round to head back down, get the hell out of here.

The sound of the door of the apartment facing the stairwell starting to open—the very door he'd been about to approach—made him pause. He turned back, not wanting to, but turning anyway. As he did so a gasp sounded.

Shock. Dismay.

Frozen in the open doorway was Eliana. And she was pushing a child's buggy.

Faintness drummed through Eliana. It could not be—she was imagining things, creating a mirage out of her own mind.

Her vision dimmed—then cleared.

He stepped up to her. Leandros. Out of nowhere.

'How...?' Her voice was as faint as the faintness drumming through her.

'A private investigator located you for me. Followed you back from the supermarket you work in.'

There was no expression in Leandros's voice. But she knew that shock must be going through him, as it was her. Knew why.

His eyes dropped from her to the buggy she was clinging to. To the infant within.

A single word broke from Leandros, and his eyes flashed
back to her. 'Yours?'

There was nothing in his voice. And yet there was everything in it. She didn't answer. Could not. Desperation
clawed in her head.

What to answer——? What to say—?

A voice called from inside the apartment.

'Who is it, Eliana?'

There was a note of fear in the voice, and she knew why.
She turned her head, called back, wanting to reassure.

'It's all right—'

But a hand was closing over the handle of the buggy.
Leandros had stepped forward, blocking her.

'Inside,' he said.

It was not a request or a suggestion.

Numbly, she drew back indoors. Her mind was in
free-fall—but how could it not be?

He followed her in. Looked past the narrow entrance
hall into the living room beyond.

Incomprehension in his face.

Slowly…very slowly…Leandros took in what he was seeing.
A living room with a dining table by the window, a little
balcony beyond. The room was filled with old-fashioned
furniture, sideboards and cupboards heavy with ornaments,
pictures on the wall, a settee covered with a crochet throw,
and another swathing a commodious armchair in which a
grey-haired woman was sitting, a walking stick propped up
beside her chair. Beyond the living room, Leandros could
see a small galley kitchen.

The grey-haired woman was speaking, sounding both alarmed and confused. Her local Macedonian accent was distinct to his ears.

'Eliana, who is this? Why is he here?'

He turned his attention to the woman. 'I am a…a friend of Eliana's, *kyria*,' he said. 'I am sorry to disturb you—but I need to speak to Eliana.'

'She was about to take Miki to the park,' the elderly woman said.

'Miki?' Leandros echoed.

His eyes went back to the infant. Maybe two years old, or three—he didn't know much about the ages of small children. The little boy was looking at him with interest in his dark eyes.

'My grandson,' the woman said.

There was pride in her voice—and doting affection too.

'We can still go to the park, Ya-Ya.'

Eliana's voice made Leandros turn back to her. She was as white as a ghost, her hands tightly gripping the handle of the buggy.

She looked at Leandros.

He nodded. Absolutely nothing here made sense. But getting out of there did.

He gave a brief, perfunctory smile to the grey-haired woman, just to be civil, and then he was turning back into the entrance lobby, reopening the front door that he had closed. Pointedly waiting for Eliana to precede him.

'We'll take the lift,' he said.

Eliana, her heart thudding as it had been from the moment her eyes had seen Leandros, sat on a bench in the little park that was only a street away from the apartment.

It was a pretty enough place, with mulberry trees for shade, pleasant paths, well-planted flower-beds, hibiscus shrubs, and an area of grass, dry and brown in this season after summer. There was a children's play area, with swings and slides, a little roundabout and a see-saw, and a few other attractions to appeal to small children. Miki was seated on one—a colourful pony perched on a strong steel spring, rocking himself happily backwards and forwards. Rubberised flooring meant that even falling off would not be painful.

Leandros sat down beside her.

Memory pierced. How they sat side by side that afternoon in the Luxembourg gardens, into which this little urban park would have fitted a score of times over, eating their *patisserie*, watching the Parisians and the tourists enjoying themselves.

'So talk,' said Leandros at her side.

His voice was grim. And, as before, it was not a request or an invitation.

For a moment she did not answer. Her eyes rested on the little boy, oblivious to the complications and currents swirling all around him.

'I take it he's yours.'

Leandros's voice was flat. Hard. As hard as stone. Things were starting to make sense—but darkly. Bleakly.

'But who the hell is his father? Because the woman in that apartment is *not* Damian's mother! And besides—' He broke off. 'Damian was gay, so—'

He broke off again.

Eliana turned to look at him. He was frowning.

'But you were a virgin,' he said. 'So how—?'

He took a rasping breath.

'IVF might have got you pregnant by Damian, or by any other man, but to give birth and still be a virgin…? Is it even *possible*?' He lifted a hand, then dropped it like lead. 'Caesarean delivery?'

He gave a swift shake of his head in negation.

'But you have no scar.' His frown deepened. 'Maybe you used a surrogate? Because how the hell else—?'

It was time for her to speak. What else could she do now? Only the truth would answer him.

'Miki is not my son.' She spoke quietly, the words falling slowly from her lips. 'He is Damian's.'

She didn't look at Leandros, only at the little boy still rocking on his pony, humming away to himself.

'Damian was not gay, as you supposed,' she said, and she knew that now she had no choice but to tell all—to tell everything. 'And as I let you think. He was just in love with someone else. Miki's mother, Maria. He wanted to marry her, but she worked as a maid in his father's house— that was how they met. Jonas, as you know, is a self-made man—and he was ambitious, as many such men are, for his only son. His heir. The last thing he would have permitted was his son throwing himself away on a woman who worked as a maid. Someone from the same background he himself had climbed away from. He wanted better for his son. He wanted old money…the prestige of a "good family". Mine, as it happened.'

She swallowed.

'That was why he found Damian's marriage to me acceptable. Oh, he profited materially too, by buying up my poor father's debts and ending up with his house. But my real value to him was that I made a very "suitable" wife for Damian socially.'

Her gaze rested on Damian's little son.

'That was Damian's father's reason for wanting me to marry Damian. Mine...' her voice twisted '...you already know.'

She drew another breath—a difficult one.

'As for Damian... Well, it suited him too. Marriage to me meant he could continue his liaison with Maria, the woman he'd never be allowed to marry. She became pregnant...gave birth to Miki. Damian, of course, could never acknowledge him—never do anything but conceal his existence, conceal Maria's as well. As for me... I knew from the start and went along with it, what Damian wanted of me—being a smokescreen to hide Maria behind, and placating his father with a marriage that Jonas would welcome. We agreed to it before we married.'

Her voice changed.

'I pitied Damian...felt for him. His father ruled him with a rod of iron. Damian was cowed by him—he always had been. He had no money of his own—his father held the purse strings. If he'd left me for Maria his father would have cut him off penniless. So he just made the best of it—as did I.'

She paused again. Then finished the sad and sorry tale.

'Maria was in the car when Damian crashed it. They died together. Leaving Miki with only his widowed grandmother. And me.'

She looked at Leandros.

'I can't abandon him, Leandros. His grandmother is getting on—you saw that. And she isn't in the best of health either. She has her pension, but it isn't much. I...I give her as much as I can afford from the meagre allowance Jonas makes me as Damian's widow, but it doesn't go very far. It stretches so far as paying for a childminder for Miki, because his grandmother can't really cope on her own. And after Damian and Maria were killed, I...I steered clear. Not because I wanted to, but because—'

She took a sharp, incising breath.

'Leandros, Jonas must never learn of his grandson's existence! He's never suspected it, and it must stay that way! Thankfully, the ambulance crew at the scene of Damian's car crash got Maria out first—she was still alive, I discovered—and she was taken to the ER. She died en route. So far as Jonas knows there was no passenger with Damian. But if he learnt about Miki he'd get hold of him! He'd value him now, because—illegitimate or not, and despite who his mother was—he's all the progeny he's going to have! He'd use his wealth and influence to get custody... ensure Miki's grandmother never saw him again. It would be a hellish childhood for Miki! I know that from what Damian said about his own childhood, and I've seen for myself—experienced for myself—how Jonas treats people. Miki is much better off with Maria's mother, despite her age and her not being well off. She adores him, and for her... Well, he's all she's got now, with her daughter dead.'

She fell silent. The tale was so sad...so pitiful all round.

'Ellee!'

The sound of Miki finally tiring of riding the pony made her get to her feet.

She went over to him, lifted him off. 'What shall we do next?' she asked brightly. Fondly.

Spending more time with him had been the one clear bonus of moving in with his grandmother in order to save on her own rent, as she now had to do. She might only be

Miki's stepmother—or not even that—but he was growing in her affections. And she in his.

'Slide! Slide!' he cried out, and she laughed, taking his hand to make their way across to the smaller of the two slides.

She hefted him up to the top, holding him steady. 'Ready?'

'Slide! Slide!' he enthused again.

'Whee!' she said, sliding him down, holding him around the waist to keep him steady.

'Again! Again!' he cried.

She moved to heft him up again. He was quite a weight, at just gone three years old.

'Let me,' said another voice.

Leandros was walking towards them.

'Right, then, young man,' he said, and swung Miki back up to the top of the slide, copying Eliana's safety precautions as Miki glided gleefully to the bottom.

It took a while for him to get bored, but he did eventually, and progressed on to the roundabout, and then an infant swing with an encased seat to stop him falling off. Finally, the sandpit beckoned, and Eliana extracted a small plastic bucket and spade from under the buggy, settling him down with them in the sand. He got stuck in happily, fully absorbed.

Benches surrounded the sandpit, most filled with mothers watching their children in the sandpit, but one was unoccupied. She sat down on it, Leandros beside her.

He turned towards her.

'What do I say to you?' he said.

'What do I say to you?'

The words—as inane as they were inadequate—echoed in his head.

When she had so shockingly revealed her virginity he hadn't known what to say to her. Nor did he know what to say now—with this even more shocking revelation.

That the 'someone else' she had gone to was Miki...

And that her marriage was a farce—a lie from the very start. A lie both she and Damian agreed to. And now she has taken responsibility for a child that is not hers. A child she will not abandon and is determined to care for—whatever it costs her. Even it costs her me...costs her what we found again in Paris.

His gaze went to the small boy, playing happily in the sand. He was a nice little lad—cheerful and sunny—and Leandros watched him happily and assiduously fill his bucket with sand, then chortle as he emptied it all out again, only to repeat the process industriously.

A thought came to him, poignant and powerful.

What if he'd been ours—Eliana's and mine?

They might easily have had a child that age by now... possibly another baby as well. His eyes went to Eliana, emotion snaking through him at what he had just thought. A sense of waste smote him.

How different our lives might have been from what they are.

She spoke now. 'There isn't really anything to say.'

Her voice was even, but he could hear a note of resignation in it. Or was it rather acceptance? Or both?

'It's just how things have panned out. We make our decisions in life, Leandros—and live with the consequences.'

She dropped her eyes, letting them go to where the little boy for whom she had shouldered a responsibility she should not have had to take on was innocently playing. A callous fate had imposed it on her.

'I can't abandon him,' she said again. 'Financially it's hard, but I'm just about managing.' She paused, glanced back at Leandros, then away again. 'The…the reason I left Paris so abruptly…' he could hear a sense of strain in her voice '…was that Maria's mother, Agnetha, had phoned me in a panic. She'd had a letter from her landlord, raising her rent or threatening her with eviction. She was so upset and scared because it was beyond her means to find the extra money, and I knew I had to get back and help out.'

She drew breath and ploughed on.

'I was already completely stretched financially, and I had to raid my savings, such as they are, to find the extra rent due. I made the decision that I could only stay afloat if I gave up my own apartment and moved in with Agnetha. It's risky—because, as I said, I don't want there ever to be any association between the widow of Damian Makris and a small child. It might start gossip, questions, speculation… and that might filter back to Jonas.'

She gave a wan smile. 'Ironically, if he jumps to the same conclusion you did, it would keep Miki safer. Jonas would just think I'd cheated on Damian and had an affair with someone else and a secret baby. Of course he'd cut off my widow's allowance instantly, but at least he wouldn't get any suspicions about Miki's true parentage.'

She fell silent again. Then spoke once more.

'I've stopped sending him to the childminder, to save some money, and cut my own working hours down, so it's only mornings. My income is less, but it was only going on the childminder anyway. This way I can bring in a little more money, and Agnetha can manage half a day looking after Miki—at least for now. I take over at lunchtime.

As I say, we're…we're just about managing…even with the rent hike.'

Frustration bit in Leandros. 'Eliana, you can't go on like this! It just isn't—'

A dozen terms for what it wasn't rang in his head, but he only picked one of them.

'Sustainable,' he said heavily. 'You can't live like this.'

She gave a little shrug. 'It's the best I can manage,' she said.

She took a breath and he felt, with a start, the lightest and briefest of touches on his wrist.

'Leandros, I'm sorry that you've found out about all of this. And I'm sorry I just walked out on you as I did in Paris. But I just didn't want you to get…well, *involved*, I guess. Sucked in.'

She got to her feet, looked down at him.

'I'd better get Miki home—Ya-Ya will have his tea ready. Don't…don't come with me. There's no point—truly.'

There was a sadness in her face that tugged at him.

'I've made my life, Leandros—and it is what it is. But…'

She took a breath, and something changed in her eyes that tugged at him even more.

'But I will always, always remember our time in Paris! I will treasure it dearly. I didn't think I would—I thought, originally, it was simply something I owed you, because of how I'd treated you when I broke our engagement and became the faithless fiancée you've always—justifiably—considered me. I knew the depth of your bitterness…your contempt for me…and how could I disagree with it, after treating you as I had? But then… Well, all that changed, didn't it? I don't really know why—and I don't deserve that it did. That you should have been so kind to me, like

I said out on the balcony that evening. But I'm grateful…
truly I am. So grateful for those wonderful days we had—'

She broke off, her face working suddenly, and then, as
if with an immense effort of will, she cleared it. She bent
down, in a sudden, swift gesture, and he felt her lips graze
his cheek, as lightly as a feather.

Then she turned, headed towards Miki, crouched down
beside him. He watched her speak to him, and saw the little
boy nod, and let her pick up the bucket and spade. She took
his hand, led him over to the buggy and settled him into it,
and then wheeled it off towards the park's exit.

She did not look back.

Eliana made it through the evening, but it was hard. Ago-
nisingly hard. With all her heart she wished Leandros had
not found her as he had. What could it achieve? Nothing—
only the agony of seeing him again, having him physically
so close to her again for that short space of time.

But he was gone again—as he must be. As he must stay.

Six years ago their lives had diverged, at her instiga-
tion. In Paris they had briefly—fleetingly—come together
again. She felt her heart turn over. Just enough for her to
know the truth about her own feelings. Just enough for
her to taste, for that brief time, the happiness that might
have been hers had she not made the choices she had six
years ago.

But now that time in Paris—that oasis of what might
have been—had gone as well. Their lives had diverged
again—for ever. And, yet again, she must live with the
consequences of her choices.

When Miki was in bed, and Agnetha had settled in her
chair to watch her TV programmes, Eliana slipped from

the apartment, saying she would get some fresh air, be back within the hour. Agnetha had made no remark about the visitor who had arrived on their doorstep, but Eliana had seen apprehension in her face. So she had given the woman the reassurance she knew she needed to.

'Yes, Leandros is the man I went on holiday with,' she said. That was how she'd explained it—nothing more. 'We had a lovely time, but I won't be seeing him again. My place is here, with you and Miki. You have my word.'

She heard what she had promised echoing again in her head as she caught a bus to take her to the seafront. She wanted to go there—to walk along the promenade as she had walked that evening with Leandros, after he had walked back into her life.

How much had changed.

And how little.

She stood, leaning on the balustrade, looking out over the dark sea at the lights from the city playing over its waters, hearing the noise of traffic behind, the buzz of the city. So old a city…stretching way back into classical times…changing hands so often over the course of the centuries. So many lives lived here—and hers was just one more of them.

For a long while she stood, gazing out to sea. Leandros might still be here in the city, in whatever hotel he'd booked into, or he might have taken an evening shuttle to Athens. That was more likely. Flying away, out of her life. This time for ever.

A line from a film came to her. An old Hollywood film, like the one she and Leandros had watched in Paris together…

'We'll always have Paris.'

But Paris, for her, was all that she would have...
All she would have of Leandros.
Through the long empty years ahead.

CHAPTER THIRTEEN

LEANDROS WAS BUSY. Punishingly busy. He had a lot to get done. He had lawyers on speed dial, estate agents on speed dial, and a firm of specialist financial investigators on speed dial. He needed to get things done—and fast.

Impatience drove him. And urgency.

And a determination that seared through him like rods of steel.

He was moving forward on all fronts and he would get where he wanted to be. Needed to be.

His phone rang and he snatched it up off his desk in the office—once his father's office, now his. He was now heading the company that had brought him the wealth that his father had been so keen for him to not jeopardise...not to share with a wife whose main interest in his son was his money, his coming inheritance.

'Any news?' he demanded of the caller—an estate agent this time.

Two minutes later he replaced the receiver, a look of satisfaction on his face. That box was ticked. Good. Time to move on the next one.

He picked up his phone again, spoke to his PA in the outer office. 'I need an employment agency,' he said briskly. Then spelt out his requirements, hung up the phone again.

OK, so what next? Time to chase that damn lawyer again—the one that specialised in family law. He needed answers—reliable ones—and then to set bureaucracy in motion.

So much to do.

He needed to move faster.

I've wasted six years—I won't waste a day longer than I have to.

That was the promise he'd made to himself as he'd watched Eliana walk away from him—for the third and final time.

Psychiko—Paris—and now Thessaloniki.

It wasn't going to happen again.

He speed-dialled the lawyer, ready to make sure it wouldn't.

I said I'd fight for her—and that's what I'm doing. Because now I know that however venal the reason she left me six years ago, this time it could not be more different.

And because of that knowledge searing through him, he would fight for her—and this time he would win.

Because now I know with absolute certainty that my whole life depends on it—my whole future.

And Eliana's.

The woman he now knew, with that same absolute certainty, he could not live without.

Eliana was in the kitchen, washing up Miki's tea things. Miki himself was snuggled up with his *ya-ya*, watching a cartoon with her. Eliana could hear their chuckles, and it warmed her. This was what she had shaped her life around—that orphaned little boy and his bereft grandmother, victims of a fate that had stripped Miki of his parents, his *ya-ya* of her only child.

I took this on—I must see it through.

The problem was brutal: lack of money. If she had more money then she could move Miki and his grandmother out of the city—install them in a little house somewhere, with a garden, space for a growing boy. But there was no money for any of that—only just enough for keeping their heads above water as it was.

Would Leandros think her impoverished, penny-pinching life now her just desserts for what she'd done six years ago? He'd been shocked by Miki's existence, but would he think it was simply up to her to deal with it? After all, he'd let her walk away—had made no attempt to come after her. Had simply accepted what she'd told him and left her to it.

She gave an inner sigh. She must not think about Leandros. He was gone from her life, and that was all there was to it. She had a life here to get on with—such as it was.

She put Miki's dried dishes away and fetched some vegetables from the fridge to make a start on supper. Her days were very much the same—a routine she was getting used to. She got on well enough with Miki's grandmother, though they had little in common other than Miki.

A sliver of apprehension went through her. Living here with Miki and Agnetha did increase the risk that word might somehow get back to Damian's father...

The sound of the doorbell made her jump, as if she had conjured up the very thing she feared. Frowning, she went back into the living room, glancing at Agnetha and Miki, still absorbed in watching their cartoon.

She unlocked the apartment door, pulling it open.

And stopped dead.

It was Leandros.

'Hello, Eliana.'

Leandros made his voice even, as if turning up on her doorstep was an unexceptional circumstance.

She was staring at him, her hand flying to her throat, shock on her face.

'May I come in?' he asked.

Numbly, she stood aside, and he walked in.

In the living room, he nodded politely to Miki's grandmother.

'Good evening—I am sorry to disturb you unexpectedly, but I would like to take Eliana out to dinner. I hope that will not inconvenience you?'

His entry had made both Miki and his grandmother look up. An expression of interest formed on Miki's face. And then recognition.

'That man,' he announced, pointing at Leandros.

Leandros smiled at him. 'Yes, that man who came to the park with you. You went on the slide.'

'Whee!' corroborated Miki happily.

Then he went back to watching his cartoon.

His grandmother, Leandros could see, was looking across at Eliana, an uncertain look on her face.

Then: 'You should go,' she said. 'I'll be fine with Miki.'

Leandros looked at Eliana. She was looking fraught.

'Please,' he said to her. 'I thought we might go back to that place we tried last time—the fish was good.'

She opened her mouth. 'I… I…'

'Good,' he said. 'That's settled.' He smiled. 'Do you want to get Miki to bed first? I can help if so.'

His smile encompassed Miki and his grandmother as well.

'I was about to cook dinner,' Eliana said.

Miki's grandmother shook her head. 'I'll have soup later on. You go. Go on—it will do you good.'

She sounded more encouraging now, though Leandros could see she was uneasy, and wondered why.

'It will indeed,' Leandros agreed smilingly.

He looked questioningly at Eliana.

She seemed to hesitate, as if she were trying to come up with another reason not to go with him. Then she simply turned round.

'I'll need a jacket,' she said.

She disappeared—presumably into her bedroom—and emerged a moment later with a short jacket. A cheap one, from a chain store, like the trousers and jumper she was wearing. Her hair was tied in a knot on the back of her head, and she wore no make-up.

Yet she is as beautiful as the moon and the stars...

His expression softened. 'Right, then, off we go.'

He bade Miki's grandmother a courteous goodbye, saying he would not keep Eliana out late, and let Eliana lead the way out of the apartment. She said not a word, and nor did he, as they went downstairs.

Out on the pavement the air was cool—autumn was reaching here too. The taxi he'd come in was waiting at the kerb, and he gave the driver their destination as he ushered Eliana into her seat, coming in after her. She sat looking out of the window, not speaking. He let her be.

The taxi gained the seafront and cruised down it till they reached the restaurant, then pulled up. Leandros hadn't made a reservation, but like last time they were early, and there were plenty of tables to choose from.

But that was the only resemblance to the last time they'd been there—that and Eliana's cheap clothes.

Because everything has changed since then—changed totally and for ever.

And now there was just one more change he must to achieve…

Eliana felt dazed and weak. What was Leandros doing here? And what was *she* doing here with him? Here in the very same place where he had asked her to come to Paris with him, after walking back into her life after six long years.

As she had that time, she went numbly along with the business of ordering. The fare was just as last time, and she ordered, without even thinking about it, what she'd had before. Leandros ordered a beer for himself, and table wine for them both, and mineral water. Bread was deposited in a wicker basket, and the waiter whisked off again.

Eliana started to pick at her bread.

What was happening? *Why?*

She lifted her head to Leandros, who was thanking the waiter as he returned with his beer and set down a carafe of red wine at the same time with her mineral water.

'Why are you here, Leandros? What is this about?'

Her tone was calm, which was odd, because inside she wasn't calm at all. Inside, emotions were ricocheting around inside her like random gunfire from every direction.

Leandros set down his beer, looked across at her. 'I've been busy,' he said.

She frowned. What did that mean?

'There was a lot to get done, but I think I've covered everything.' He paused, then spoke again. 'Starting, I think, with this.'

He reached inside his jacket pocket, drew out a long envelope and set it down in front of her.

'Open it,' he instructed.

The frown still on her face, she did so. Her hands seemed clumsy, her fingers making a hash of opening it neatly. She yanked out the thick paper inside, unfolded it. Stared.

Not understanding.

Not understanding at all.

'It's the deeds to your father's house,' Leandros said.

Her eyes flew to him, distended.

'I bought it from Jonas Makris,' he told her. 'Oh, he didn't know it was me—I used a proxy. A very eager proxy,' he said with a wry expression on his face. 'He offered him an absurdly high price—saying how he adored houses of that period and was determined to acquire it, whatever the cost. Jonas couldn't resist—though I did tussle him down from the price he thought he could get,' he said with a note of satisfaction audible in his voice. 'I made speed of the essence, and the transaction went through yesterday. So...' his voice changed '...there it is. Your father's house, back in the family.'

He paused, clearly seeing the shock, the incomprehension, in her face.

'It's yours, Eliana,' he said.

Her eyes distended again. Not with incomprehension now, but in disbelief—swiftly followed by the shaking of her head.

'No, of course it isn't! Of course it isn't mine! It's yours—*yours*, Leandros! *You* bought it, with *your* money—of course it's yours!'

It was his turn to shake his head. 'What would I want with a house like that? I've got a perfectly good one of my own in Psychiko. Left to me by my father.' His voice changed again. 'Just as *your* father, Eliana, should have left you his house.' A hardness entered his voice. 'And not expected you to marry a man like Damian Makris to stop him losing it!'

Eliana bit her lip. 'He didn't, Leandros. He didn't expect me to do it. Never. I married Damian of my own free will—it was my choice. I told you that.' Her voice dropped. 'Just as it was my choice to break my engagement to you to do so. My choice—mine alone.' There was a tightness in her voice as she looked at him. 'I married money, Leandros—and it was my choice to do so.'

'To save your father's house for him.' That edge was still in his voice. 'To save him from financial ruin.'

Her expression changed. 'But my marriage to Damian also kept me from poverty—just like you've always thrown at me. The poverty you've always said I could not have faced had your father disinherited you as he threatened.'

She lifted her chin as she spoke. She could make no defence against Leandros's accusation—his accusation six years ago and his accusation ever since.

A flash came in his eyes. Anger. Well, she deserved that. She always had.

But his anger was not for that reason.

'That,' he bit out, 'is not true.'

He reached for his beer, took a hefty swallow of it, set it back on the table with a thud. That flash in his eyes came again.

'I've thrown it at you time and time again! And it's never been true! Because if it were—if all you cared about was a luxury lifestyle—you wouldn't be living the life you're leading now. The life I found you living the first time I tracked you down to that dump you lived in. And you're facing poverty now, taking on Damian's child as you have—'

'I don't have much choice,' she replied.

She didn't want this conversation. There was no point to it—no point at all.

The flash was there again. Fiercer still.

'Yes, you do have a choice! You could leave Miki and his grandmother to fend for themselves. And if Jonas gets hold of his grandson, what is that to you?'

'I'll never do that—never!' There was vehemence in her voice.

'Exactly! And that proves my point. You could take the allowance Jonas makes you and keep it all for yourself.' His voice twisted. 'Keep all those damn clothes I bought you in Paris! Head back to Athens, get out and about again—find another husband or a lover. It doesn't matter which. Your incredible beauty would guarantee you hit paydirt!'

Her face was paling, the blood draining from it. Dear God, did he still think that of her?

His voice changed. 'But you won't. It's unthinkable to you.' He took a razored breath. 'As unthinkable as you marrying Damian just to keep that luxe lifestyle for yourself.' A laugh broke from him, harsh and humourless. 'Because you didn't marry him for that reason at all, even though it was what I told myself, and went on telling myself these past six years. I wanted a reason to hate you, because you no longer valued my love! And that hurt, Eliana—dear God, it hurt! I saw you as pampered and cosseted by your father—overprotected. But it was the other way round—that's what I've finally realised! It was you protecting your father. That's why you married Damian—to protect your father, to let him see out his days in the house he loved, to escape the financial ruin he was facing at least for his lifetime. You were landed with it after his death instead. Just like your husband landed you with the son he was too scared to claim for himself!'

'Don't blame them!' Her cry came from the heart. 'Don't blame Damian—please don't! He was so cowed by his father—so scared of him. And my father just wasn't good with money. Those with inherited money often aren't good—they weren't the ones who made it, and they don't know how to manage it. He…he did his best. But he just… well, got into a mess. And after my mother died he was so devastated…'

Leandros was looking at her. 'I thought you cossetted… overprotected by a doting father. But I'll say it again: it was the other way round—wasn't it, Eliana?'

She looked away. The truth was hard to face—she had loved her father so dearly…

'He was a good man—a kind man—but…but unworldly. He didn't even see how Damian's father was netting him, getting control over what happened to the house. And the stress of losing all his money had already given him one stroke…'

Her gaze dropped to where the deeds to the villa lay on the table in front of her.

'I'm glad,' she said slowly, sadly, 'that he never realised he was going to lose the house when he died…that it wouldn't come to me.'

She heard Leandros speak. 'But now it has.'

Her eyes flashed up. 'You know I can't possibly accept it! How could I? And what possible reason could you have for giving it to me?'

There was a veiling of his eyes. Yet they still rested on her like weights.

'Do you not know, Eliana? Do you really not know?'

His words fell into silence. Around her she could hear noise from the kitchen, hear the waiter greeting the other diners starting to arrive, conversations beginning.

Could hear, inside her, the thudding of her heart. Which was like a hammer. Drumming in her pulse.

'I want it,' he spoke slowly and clearly, for all the veiling in his eyes, 'to be my wedding present to you, Eliana.'

The drumming was deafening...drowning out everything. Making her feel faint. Making the room come and go around her.

She felt her hand taken, lifted. Heard Leandros speak again, his voice low. And what was in it was an intensity that broke her apart.

'Six years ago you walked away from me, turned me down. This time—' his fingers around hers spasmed '—don't. Just...don't. Don't turn me down again.' He paused, then spoke again, his voice husky, as if each word were painful. 'I couldn't bear it.'

Her face worked. Emotion was storming up in her, storming through the drumming of her blood. Leandros was speaking again, his words breaking through the deafening drumming of her blood, reaching for her. Finding her. Emotion was filling his words...so much emotion...

'We found each other again in Paris. Don't— Eliana *don't* let us lose each other again! When you walked out on me that second time, it was like...it was like a knife in my throat. And I knew...*knew*...that what we'd first had, all those years ago, was there again.' His voice dropped.

'Maybe it had never gone away. Just been suffocated by my bitterness...'

She turned her fingers in his. Then she spoke, her voice low and halting—and painful.

'I hurt you. I hurt you and I know I did. And I have never, for a single day, forgiven myself. I told you in Paris that, given a second chance, I'd make the same choice again— marry Damian. Because nothing would have been different if that second chance had come. If I hadn't married Damian my father would still have been facing a financial ruin I could not have borne to impose on him, and—'

She stopped.

His expression had changed. Arrested.

'And what?' There was an edge in his voice, but the blade was not aimed at her.

She shut her eyes. That drumming was still in her ears, her heart, her pulse.

'And your father would still have been threatening to disinherit you if you married me,' she said.

Her eyes flew open. Suddenly it was her hand clenching his, crushing it with her intensity.

'Leandros, did you never think how I felt when he told me that? Told me you'd be penniless if you married me? Dear God, Leandros, I *loved* you! How could I possibly have gone on with marrying you knowing it would estrange you from your father? Strip you of your inheritance? How could I have done that to you?'

He was staring at her. She wanted to cry out—cry out the dismay she'd felt when his father had made it so crystal-clear to her what marrying his son would do to Leandros.

'So I didn't, Leandros. I didn't do it to you. I told you

I didn't want to marry you any longer and I let you say... let you say...'

'Let me call you what I did. Venal and luxury-loving— another Manon.' His voice was hollow. Shaken.

'It was better that you did that. Better that you hated and despised me than felt I was only marrying Damian to protect my father. If you hated and despised me you could move on—set me aside.'

He let go her hand and it felt cold suddenly. But not as cold as the chill that filled her as he spoke again. Slowly, heavily. As if a weight were on his chest.

He drew a breath—a razored one. 'My father only said that to test you. He'd warned me ever since I was a teenager that there would be women out there whose interest would not be in me, but my family's wealth. He'd told me he would test any woman I wanted to marry. Test her to see what her reaction was. And I—I agreed with it.'

His voice grew heavier yet.

'I told myself that your rejection of me justified that test, justified his suspicions—proved that they were not groundless. He told me that your father was in financial difficulties, that your marrying me would be a good way out of them. And when you walked out on me I thought he was right. And then, when your engagement to Damian Makris was announced, I knew it for certain. Money, and only money, was your reason for marrying—marrying anyone at all.'

He reached for his beer, his fingers indenting around the glass such that the tips whitened. He knocked back the rest of it. Placed the empty glass back on the table. Eyes spearing hers.

'I have never,' he said, 'been more wrong in my life.'

He passed a hand over his brow, as if in a weariness very profound.

'I screwed it up. I screwed it up so totally, so completely. And if I hadn't—if I'd trusted you…trusted the love I knew you felt for me—I would have refused to believe your reasons for leaving me. Challenged them—demolished them somehow. I would have—*should* have—realised why you were saying those things to me.'

She shook her head. 'But I still wouldn't have married you if it had meant your disinheritance, your estrangement from your father.'

He thudded his hand down on the table. 'But it wouldn't have! I told you—he was just testing you, that's all! If you'd stuck by me, told me you didn't care if I were rich or poor, then he—and I—would have known that it was me you loved, not the Kastellanos money! Oh, God, Eliana, we'd have bailed out your father—rescued him—and then you and I…' his voice was raw '…we would have spent these last six years together—as man and wife. The way we should have done if I hadn't screwed it up. The way…'

His voice changed, and he reached for her hand again, seizing it as if it were a treasure that was about to slip away, out of his grasp.

'The way we still can.'

That razored breath came again.

'Marry me, Eliana—marry me this time around. With all the past cleared out of the way! Paris proved it to us both!'

His voice dropped, filled now with an intensity that reached into her very being.

'It proved to me that I have never, never stopped loving you. I tried to—tried to kill it, poison it, defile it. But in Paris it broke free of all that. Even if I still hadn't realised it, every night with you proved it—every day! And if—oh, dear God—*if,* my most beloved Eliana, in that heart of yours which has made you make such sacrifices, you can find a grain, a seed, a crumb of what you once felt for me, then... Oh, then I will spend all my life—*all my life!*—growing it in you.'

Her vision was clouding. There was an upwelling within her that was unstoppable.

'You don't have to do that, Leandros,' she said. Her voice was almost a whisper, broken in its intensity. 'Because it's there—it's always been there. Always! I thought it had gone—told myself that the only reason I'd agreed to go to Paris with you was because I owed it to you after all I'd done to you. But it was a lie! Oh, it was a lie. And when... when we came together, in each other's arms, then I knew what the truth was. I was with you, in your arms, for one reason only—because I still loved you. I love you and I always will, Leandros... Always and always and always...'

Her vision had gone completely. Tears were running down her cheeks. Her heart was turning over and over within her.

She clutched at his hand and he lifted it—lifted it to his lips, crushing it with his kiss. She gazed at him with her obliterated vision, tears still streaming. Her heart overflowing even more than her eyes.

A discreet cough sounded beside her. She looked dimly in its direction. Their waiter was silently offering her a stack of paper serviettes. She gave a laugh—a broken, emotional sound—and grabbed them, using one, then two and three, because her tears would not stop. They would not stop for there were six long years of tears to shed...

She heard Leandros speak—but not to her. He was addressing the waiter.

'I think,' he was saying, 'that she's giving me a positive answer to my marriage proposal...'

The waiter was nodding. 'Oh, quite definitely. My wife cried all day when I asked her to marry me! It's their way of showing happiness, you know,' he said kindly.

He disappeared, and Eliana went on crying. She could not stop. Leandros was crushing her hand, and she was clinging to it. Clinging to it as if were life itself. Which to her it was.

Then the waiter was there again, a bottle in his hand.

'Compliments of the house, the chef says. He's the owner, so what he says goes.'

He put the bottle on the table. It was sparkling wine, a popular Greek domestic variety, and he was removing the cage, then easing the cork. He poured them two glasses—wine glasses, meant for the wine in the carafe. But that was fine by her, because everything was fine by her—everything...

'Congratulations!' said the waiter, and disappeared again.

Leandros was picking up his glass, tapping it against hers. So she picked hers up as well.

'To us,' he said. 'And to you, Eliana, the heart of my heart, whom I let go and have grieved for ever since. And now I claim you again—with all my heart.'

He clinked his glass against hers again and shakily, tearfully, she raised hers to her lips.

'To us,' she echoed.

For finally, after six anguished years, there was an 'us'.

It was finally true.

And now it always would be.
Always.

Hand in hand, they strolled along the wide Thessaloniki seafront. They were not the only ones to do so, but to each other only they existed. A great peace filled Leandros. A peace of the heart, and of the mind, and of the soul itself.

Regret filled him, yes, and he knew it always would—for what he'd done six years ago, to himself and Eliana. Condemning them to the wasted years between. And yet for all that, far more overwhelming was the thankfulness that poured through him.

He paused, turning Eliana towards him now.

'There's a line somewhere in Shakespeare's *Othello*, about how Othello "threw a pearl away"—and that is what I did. I threw you away…let you leave me without a fight… because I did not trust you—did not trust the love I *knew* you felt for me.'

He drew a breath, his eyes holding hers. They would never let her go again. 'But I will trust it for ever now—and you, my heart, my love, can trust for ever, and for all eternity, my love for you.'

In the lamplight, he could see tears welling in her eyes, and he bent to kiss them away. Then he kissed her mouth as well. She slipped her hand from his, but only to wind it around his waist, strong, possessive.

His hands went to her shoulders. He lifted his mouth away, his eyes still pouring into hers. 'Forgive me.'

His voice was low and husky. His eyes were saying all that that brief plea could not.

A cry broke from her, and her arms tightened around his waist.

'Oh, my dearest, dearest one—we've been given each other again, and that is a gift past any price.' A crooked smile curved her lips. 'Even that of any pearl…'

He gave a laugh, releasing her shoulders. 'You shall have pearls and rubies and diamonds and emeralds and sapphires and—'

She kissed him, and it silenced him. Then she spoke again.

'Leandros…money—the want of it, the fear of it—drove us apart. With all my heart—with *all* my heart—I wish it had not been so. Had you been a poor man six years ago, and had my father always been poor, such that there would have been no call for me to protect him as I felt I had to do, then *nothing* would have stopped me marrying you. Believe me, I beg of you, that is the truth.'

It was his turn to kiss her, so he did. Gently and tenderly.

'Always,' he said.

He smiled down at her lovingly. Then his smile turned rueful.

'How I wish,' he said, 'that I hadn't promised Miki's grandmother I wouldn't keep you out late. All I want to do now…' his voice was husky, and she knew why '…is whisk you off to my hotel room and make passionate love to you until dawn breaks.'

She gave a laugh, her hands tightening around him. 'Me too,' she said. 'But first I must get back, sit down with Agnetha and talk with her.' Her expression changed. 'Are you sure, Leandros, that you're happy with what you told me at the restaurant? About your plans for how we should settle matters?'

He kissed the tip of her nose—it was safer than kissing her lips, given that he could not, alas, whisk her back to his hotel room.

'Absolutely. It will work out perfectly for all of us.' A thought struck him. 'Shall we take her and Miki out to lunch tomorrow and tell her together? We both know a good local fish restaurant here—and after our free bottle of fizz, I think we owe them some more custom.'

She laughed again. 'But you insisted they put it on the bill—*and* left a huge tip too!'

'Well, happiness makes you do things like that,' he answered.

He would have bought a hundred bottles of domestic sparkling wine if it would have given him even a fraction of a fraction of the happiness that was possessing his whole being now.

He lifted her hands away from his waist—that was safer too...not to have her crushed against him. He slipped his hand into hers instead. Started walking forward again, along the seafront.

How long it had taken for him to arrive here—thanks to his own blindness and lack of trust, his fear and bitterness. But now he was here, holding the hand of the woman he loved—the woman he had always loved, would always love, till the last breath in his body and beyond—and no power in heaven or earth was going to separate them again.

'My Eliana,' he said, pausing to kiss her one more time.

And his name was breathed by her in turn, with all the love in it that was in him for her...sighed in the gentle breath of the soft breeze lifting off the night-dark sea as they walked forward again, hand in hand, into the future that awaited them—waited them to possess it together.

EPILOGUE

ELIANA SAT BACK on the sun lounger. Leandros's was drawn up beside her, and both were shaded by a parasol against the warm early-summer sun. A little way away Miki was sitting in the shallow paddling pool that had now been added to the villa's main pool. He was perfectly content, splashing away, playing with his fleet of colourful plastic boats, chatting to them.

Eliana smiled to see him. He was happy here—and so was his beloved *ya-ya*. Both had made the transition to her father's villa—now hers and Leandros's out-of-city home where they came for weekends.

They often invited guests like Chloe and her new husband, Andreas—Chloe had been delighted at her reconciliation with Leandros.

Miki and his *ya-ya* lived in the little lodge where her father's housekeeper had once lived. Keeping them company was Sophie, who combined the roles of nanny for Miki and home help for his grandmother.

Hiring Sophie had been part of what had kept Leandros so busy before he'd descended on Eliana in Thessaloniki to lift her from that life into the life he wanted for her—as his beloved and adored wife. And as Eliana wanted Leandros for her beloved and adored husband, it suited them both.

And there was more that had kept Leandros busy then, which was bearing fruit now. Beyond the hiring of Sophie, and the repurchasing of Eliana's father's villa, his lawyer and his specialist financial investigator had been busy.

His lawyer had set in train Miki's grandmother's claim for formal adoption—which had gone through, with Eliana and Leandros named as guardians. Now Miki, Eliana knew with relief, would be safe from Damian's father, should he ever discover he had a grandson.

As for the financial investigator—Leandros had told her what he had found out.

'However closely Jonas had controlled Damian, it seemed odd to me that, with his having been so tragically killed in a car crash, there had not been some kind of life insurance pay-out. Well, there had—and I've been given proof of it. And proof of something more. The beneficiary, Eliana, was not Damian's father. It was you—his wife. His widow. It's a generous sum—a very generous one. Jonas kept it from you, but you have the legal claim on it—you can get it back.'

She had. But not for herself.

'This is for Miki,' she'd told Leandros. 'His father's legacy. Invest it for me, make it grow, and it will be his inheritance—set him on his way when he's grown.'

She had been glad to do it—it had been the right thing to do.

For herself she had so much.

I have everything—I have Leandros. He is all I could ever want—rich, poor, or anything in between. Because now he is mine.

And she was his—now and for ever…for ever and now.

Her gaze went to him, the man she loved with all her heart and soul and always had.

He felt her gaze upon him and looked across at her.

'It will be Miki's birthday soon,' he mused. 'Four years old.'

He paused. Let his eyes rest on Eliana. There was speculation in them, and something more—something that made her heart turn over. As it so often did whenever he looked at her for any reason at all.

'It could be time,' he said slowly, 'for him to have a stepbrother or stepsister. Sadly, he'll always be an only child—but we can provide him with step-siblings. He'd like that.'

She reached for his hand. 'He would,' she said, 'and so would I—and so would you. This house cries out for children—and I was so very happy here as a child.'

Leandros lifted her hand and casually bestowed a kiss upon it. 'Then it's settled,' he said. 'One stepbrother or stepsister coming up—the moment nature can provide it.'

Eliana laced her fingers through his, letting her thumb stroke languorously across his palm.

'Nature might need a helping hand,' she said lazily, suggestively. 'A romantic setting might do the trick. What do you think?'

She eyed Leandros. He took the bait, just as she knew he would. They ran in harmony and always would.

'Romantic setting, hmm…? Let me think…' He furrowed his brow. 'Call me predictable,' he ventured, 'but how does Paris strike you for romance?'

She gave a soft laugh. It had been their planned destination six years go, but they had never made it there. And then it had been the place where, miraculously, all the bitterness between them had been dissolved. And after that, just before Christmas, when the air had been crisp and cold, with chestnuts being roasted on braziers in the street and Christmas markets festooned with decorations, and all the great edifices of the city illuminated nightly, Paris had been where they had gone for their true honeymoon.

And now it would be their destination again.

'Paris it is,' she said contentedly.

And Leandros laughed and kissed her hand again.

Later on, when midnight approached and they retired to their bedroom and their bed, he kissed her all over—and then more than kissed her.

Afterwards, as they lay in each other's arms, heart against heart, he cradled her.

'Might as well get into practice for Paris,' he said.

And that, thought Eliana, as sleep drifted over her and she fell, as she always did in his arms, into the sweetest dreams, was an excellent idea...

* * * * *

Were you blown away
by Greek's Temporary Cinderella?

Then don't miss out on these other passion-fueled stories
by Julia James!

Destitute Until the Italian's Diamond
The Cost of Cinderella's Confession
Reclaimed by His Billion-Dollar Ring
Contracted as the Italian's Bride
The Heir She Kept from the Billionaire

Available now!

HARLEQUIN
Reader Service

Enjoyed your book?

Try the perfect subscription for Romance readers and get more great books like this delivered right to your door.

See why over 10+ million readers have tried Harlequin Reader Service.

Start with a Frec Welcome Collection with free books and a gift—valued over $20.

Choose any series in print or ebook. See website for details and order today:

TryReaderService.com/subscriptions